SUMMER'S END

HARPER BLISS

ISBN-13 978-988-12898-1-0
ISBN-10 9881289815

For Caroline, the order in my chaos.

EMILY

The Red Lodge looked much tidier than Emily had envisioned, not that she had high expectations after three months on the road. The house felt a bit out of place, perched in between resorts along the beach, as if someone had forgotten to tear it down while developing the rest of the coast. She'd been scouring the internet on her phone while in Bangkok, looking for a decent place to stay in Samui. Somewhere cheap enough so that she didn't have to ask her parents for money again, but comfortable enough to meet her not-so-modest standards. She blamed her family for surrounding her with too much luxury because the only hotels she liked were well above her fifteen-quid-a-night budget while the ones that fit into it nicely appeared way too shabby—even the pictures on their website—for a girl brought up in Holland Park.

She'd asked her parents for extra cash twice. The first time when she had run out of funds one third into her three-month journey. The second—and last, she had sworn—after she'd bought a series of paintings from an extremely talented Vietnamese artist for quite a bargain, but the shipping costs had set her back half a month in lodging. She could hardly drag three forty-eight by sixty inch canvasses with her on the rest of her trip. Determined to make it on her own for one last week— because wasn't that what this trip was all about?—she'd looked away from her phone and her gaze had landed on a pile of red flyers stacked on the nearby window sill.

The Red Lodge - Beachside B&B - Koh Samui
Only 3 rooms available at any time. Not for party people.
25 USD per night.

Tired of looking for a decent place to stay, Emily converted the amount in her head and opened the e-mail application on her phone. A few hours later she had written confirmation and a bed—although she had no idea of the state it would be in—for the last five days of her three-month sabbatical in Asia. The next day she boarded a plane to the island.

"Emily Kane?" A woman with the exact same upper-crust accent as her mother appeared in the doorway.

"That's me." It was hard to pin an age on her, but Emily guessed, based on nothing else but the similarity in tone of voice, that the woman must have been about the same age as her mother.

"Welcome to The Red Lodge. My name is Marianne." She extended her hand, which took Emily by surprise as she wasn't used to being greeted with a firm handshake anymore. "Please, come inside."

Emily quite liked the personable approach and figured that, as she was flying back to London soon, she might as well get used to British people again. Not that she hadn't encountered way too many on her travels, but she'd become rather good at avoiding them.

"Is it just you?" Marianne asked.

I'm not hiding a small person in my backpack. Emily just smiled and nodded. "Yep." Six months ago, when she was still engaged, she and Jasper had considered Thailand a viable honeymoon destination. Surely they would have visited one of the islands, but they would never have picked a low-key place like this for accommodation.

But Jasper wasn't here, and that was exactly how she wanted it. Wasn't it?

"Absolutely nothing wrong with that." Marianne flashed her a smile before proceeding to check her in.

Emily ran her eyes over the faded Ramones t-shirt— so tight around the shoulders—the woman wore and considered it quite age-inappropriate.

"Things are pretty relaxed around here. There's no set breakfast time so feel free to sleep as long as you like." Marianne handed her an old-fashioned key. "The kitchen," she curled her fingers into air quotes, "closes at ten p.m. and silence is appreciated at night."

"Thanks." Emily took the key into possession and made a mental note to store her valuables in the safe—if her room even had one.

"Let me show you to your quarters." Marianne arched her eyebrows up in mock anticipation. "You're on the ground floor, overlooking the garden."

Emily didn't quite know what to make of Marianne. The ultra-posh accent didn't seem to fit with her surroundings—nor with the t-shirt. She slung her backpack over her shoulder and followed Marianne from the hallway to the back of the house. Of all the places she'd stayed at, this one appeared the most at odds. The decoration was Asian, but the house felt thoroughly European. As though it had been transported here from Holland Park.

"Here we are." The door to the room was open and when Marianne showed her in, Emily couldn't believe what she saw. It was bright and the water from the pool outside reflected blue onto the wardrobe mirror through a large French window.

Stumped for words, Emily turned to her hostess.

"Quite a common reaction." A satisfied grin tugged at the corners of the woman's mouth. "But what can I say, I like my surroundings well-finished and pretty."

"But... twenty-five dollars?"

"I'm not in this business for the money," Marianne said matter-of-factly. "Why don't you freshen up and I'll see you later. I'll be outside."

Before Emily had a chance to reply, Marianne had turned on her heels and closed the door behind her. Emily couldn't help but wonder if she'd just had an enormous bout of luck or whether there was a catch to this lush room she had just ventured into.

MARIANNE

Another one who's trying to find herself. In the five years since Marianne had opened the Lodge to the public, she'd seen too many of them pass. She walked up the stairs to her own room on the top floor. The third step creaked, as it had been doing for the past three weeks.

Emily reminded her of a previous life—the life she had led before her self-chosen exile to Thailand. Marianne had no idea how long the girl had been travelling, but even the dark complexion of her skin and the natural highlights in her hair—both the result of hours of exposure to the hot South-East Asian sun, no doubt— couldn't hide her airs and graces.

If she's lucky, she'll learn. Marianne drew her t-shirt over her head and scanned the room for her bikini. Emily was the only guest today and a swim in the ocean was long overdue. Before swapping her undies for swimwear, Marianne dropped to the floor in front of the mirror and performed twenty-five pushups. She'd only recently started working out again and they left her puffing on the carpet for a few minutes. Despite the sudden fatigue, which she knew would pass, she felt stronger. A word she hadn't associated with herself in a long time.

After slipping into a black bikini and covering the rest of her skin with a t-shirt and pair of shorts, she descended the stairs. The house was too empty today. Even at full capacity, it was never loud or exceptionally cheerful, but at least there was some noise. Some signs of life. A pipe gurgling to life or water spattering in the pool outside. A reminder that she wasn't alone.

She trudged through the garden, along the stone path by the pool, until she reached the beach. Outside, the sun beat down mercilessly, but the sky was a blue you couldn't imagine if it wasn't staring you in the face. So deep and pristine, it should grace many a touristic pamphlet, but a picture could never fully capture its essence. The sense of freedom and joy it provoked. The healing quality of a blue sky you could always count on during certain times of year was invaluable.

The sand was hot beneath her feet, but Marianne was used to that by now. She walked a bit quicker until she reached the moist part of the beach and stood overlooking the ocean, as she did every day. The waves in August were usually lazier than this.

This was a quiet beach, with only two medium-sized resorts spread out across the strip. Marianne would never have chosen it otherwise. Not a lot of swimmers ventured into the ocean at this time of the day, preferring the shadow provided by their hotel pool gazebos over the unflinching heat of the Thai afternoon sun.

"Is the water too cold for you?"

The voice that came from behind Marianne startled her. She spun around and looked into Emily's grinning face.

"That was quick." She returned Emily's smile. "Room too small and stuffy for you?"

"Not in the least." Emily winked and ran past her with the enthusiasm of a child who's never seen the sea in her life. She wore a skimpy bikini with a flower pattern. Marianne followed her with her eyes as Emily waded into the water. Her skin was nut brown and contrasted heavily with the lightness of her hair that had grown unruly. Marianne checked herself for any signs of sudden arousal—for any inkling that some day this would pass—but as usual, she felt nothing. Hadn't done so in five years.

5

She wondered what Emily's story was—because they all had one. The ones who turned up alone despite the fact that they looked as if they'd never been anywhere on their own in their life. She looked a bit too old to be on a post-university gap year, but these days, you just never knew.

Marianne let her shorts drop onto the sand, stripped off her t-shirt and walked into the waves. It struck her again how different it was to cross from land to ocean in different parts of the world. Brighton had its charms—and she'd owned a holiday house there for ten years for a reason—but, when put in perspective, the North Sea really had nothing on the Pacific Ocean. Having it at her disposal whenever she wanted was a big plus, but it wasn't the main reason she had fled Britain. If only.

With strong strokes—at least she swam every day and swimming in waves does so much more for the upper body than counting laps in the pool—she quickly made up the distance between Emily and her. If she'd had a romantic bone left in her body, Marianne could have almost considered it a romantic moment—swimming towards another woman in the shimmering ocean. She shook off the thought and engaged in what had become her specialty since opening the Lodge. Small talk. Fleeting moments, people passing through, enough superficial connections to get through the day and feel human but not enough to ever feel deserted again. This was her life now, and it was exactly how she wanted it.

Facing Emily, Marianne treaded water. Her feet could reach the ocean floor, but she really did want to get stronger.

"How long have you been travelling?" Marianne always found it interesting to discover how people ended up here. All these people passing by, occupying a room in her house—all momentarily in the same situation, but always a different tale to tell.

EMILY

"Three months. This is my last stop. After this, I'm flying home." After the turmoil of Bangkok, this place felt like paradise. Emily didn't wait for her words to register with Marianne, who had probably heard a similar story a million times before. She let her head sink back into the water and let it cool her glowing scalp.

"And where's that?" Marianne asked as soon as Emily's ears breached the surface again. *Excellent question.* Could she just go back after having burned so many bridges? Could London ever be home again? It was a big enough city for a transformation, to change your life and move on. For something different.

"London, I guess." She shrugged, her shoulders hidden under water.

"You guess? That doesn't sound very convincing." The expression on Marianne's face changed from displaying casual interest into something more intense. *Oh great, a shrink.*

"Stuff happened before I left." Before she'd packed her bags in a hurry—in a frenzied daze, a state of emotional distress leading to tunnel vision until all she wanted to do was leave.

"I can't do it," she'd said to Jasper's flabbergasted face. "I can't marry you and have your perfect Holland Park children, one boy and one girl. One with your dark hair and one with my blonde curls. I can't see it, Jasper. It's not what I want."

"But…" Jasper, usually not stumped for words, had no recourse. "The wedding's next month."

By the time she was expected to walk down the aisle, Emily was drinking cheap beer in Hanoi, too busy avoiding the crazy traffic attacking her from all sides to think much about the significance of the day.

"It usually does." Marianne shot her a smile and ducked away from her. It didn't look as if she was going to press Emily on the subject. Emily couldn't decide if that was good or bad. She'd have to start talking about it some time. First, though, she had a few more lazy days in the sun to enjoy. She scanned the horizon—blue on blue—and understood why Marianne would choose to live here.

Marianne was making good progress against the waves. Emily watched her body transform into a small dot in the distance. Impressive, she thought, because despite loving the water, and having had the privilege of being taught by the best swimming instructors money could buy, she knew she just didn't have it in her. She didn't possess a swimmer's physique or mindset.

Emily let her body drift in the water for a while, squinting against the sun. To empty her mind of the looming journey home, she tried to recite all the titles of the books she'd read since she left. It was an ever-growing list that helped her fall asleep in noisy hostels. Not that she stayed in too many of those. It had been the initial plan—low-budget, back-to-basics living—but when push had come to shove, Emily didn't have it in her and she knew full well that, no matter what happened, her father would, in the end, always pick up her credit card bill. It's hard to live dangerously with an ever-present safety net.

After cooling off her body, Emily padded back to shore. When she looked back, she spotted Marianne swimming in her direction with swift freestyle strokes. Perhaps she had guessed wrong when she'd placed her in the same age bracket as her mother, because her mother surely couldn't do that. She had other qualities though, like looking down her nose at people. And judging by appearances.

Emily made her way back to the Lodge's garden. There was just enough room for a small pool and a patio with some lounge and regular chairs. Every single piece of furniture looked expensive, as if belonging in a five-star hotel instead of a modest guesthouse.

Marianne had been adamant about not being in the hotel service industry for the money, and by the look of things at the Red Lodge, she was hardly strapped for cash.

Before sitting down in one of the chairs under the beige sun shield, Emily grabbed a towel from a small stack next to the pool and wrapped it around her dripping body. She'd only just sat down when she heard Marianne's footsteps slap against the flat stones of the garden path. Marianne had put her t-shirt back on and it clung to her sun-bronzed flesh in wet patches. Not for the first time on this three-month trip, Emily felt a glowing heat flare somewhere in an undefinable spot beneath her skin.

First she had wanted to get away from everything, and she had, the only further place she could have gone was Australia.

"Would you like a drink?" Marianne asked, and Emily had to consciously lift her gaze from Marianne's body to her face.

"I could murder a beer." She looked up into Marianne's face. When it was backlit by the sun she could clearly make out the small wrinkles around her sparkling brown eyes.

"Coming right up." Marianne shot her a wink and Emily felt it again. It's not that she couldn't explain it— she hadn't lived that sheltered a life—it was more that she was afraid what it might do to her if she gave in.

She straightened her back and pushed the sensation away—she'd become really good at that.

MARIANNE

"If you don't mind me asking..." Marianne sat opposite Emily on the patio. "How old are you?" She'd brought an ice bucket from the kitchen holding a six-pack of Singha. They each sipped one from the bottle.

"Still young enough not to mind the question." Despite them sitting under the sun shield, a shiny glimmer caught Emily's hair. "I'm twenty-four and, as of recently, officially the black sheep of the Kane family." Emily opened her palms to the sky as if presenting herself.

"Plenty of time to turn that around then." Marianne took a swig from her beer, but kept her eyes on Emily.

Emily chuckled. "Maybe I don't want to turn it around. Maybe I've just had enough."

Marianne arched up her eyebrows in response.

"How very dramatic of me." Emily pulled one leg up onto her chair. "But people do say it's easier to talk to a stranger."

"We've seen each other in bikinis. We're hardly strangers anymore." Marianne was taken aback by the words exiting her mouth. She looked away for an instant before facing Emily again. "I'm sorry, I didn't mean to—"

"It's quite all right." Emily brushed a stray strand of hair away from her forehead. "If I could look like you when I'm your age—" Emily brought her hand to her mouth. "Gosh, now it's my turn to apologise, I mean, I don't even know how old you are," she stuttered.

Marianne wondered if the blush creeping up her cheeks was visible. She hoped not. "Forty-one on Saturday."

"Saturday?" Emily's eyes grew a little wider. "Really?" She seemed to have recovered from her earlier slip-up. "Are you having a party?"

Marianne relaxed back into her chair. "I'm not really one for celebrating anymore."

"Oh." Emily looked at her through squinted eyes.

"Besides, I'm working."

"Are you always working?" Emily placed her empty bottle on the table. "Is it just you here?"

"I employ two people to clean the rooms and do the dishes, but I manage all the rest." Not that there was so much to manage. Marianne didn't feel as if she was running a business. She considered the people who came to stay at the lodge more houseguests than customers. Sometimes, a few days went by without visitors, and that was fine by her as well. She didn't advertise The Red Lodge on the internet. Everyone who stayed here, arrived either by chance, by word-of-mouth, or because of the flyers she had delivered to a few choice establishments in Bangkok and Chiang Mai.

"What if someone has a special request?" Emily reached for another bottle of beer, uncapped it with the beer opener tied to the bucket and handed it to Marianne.

"Like what?" Marianne accepted the beer.

"A birthday cake delivery." Emily grinned at her and only now did Marianne notice how her smile dimpled her cheeks.

"I'm always very upfront with my guests about what's possible and what's not." She placed the cool bottom of the bottle on her thigh. "But if someone wants to celebrate their birthday here, they're very welcome and I will make some calls."

"God, you really are British, aren't you?" Emily mock-sighed.

"How can you possibly tell?" Marianne made an extra effort to sound as stiff and posh as possible.

Emily burst out in a little giggle before a silence fell between them.

"You must be hungry?" Marianne's caring instinct kicked in. "Shall I fix us some dinner?"

"You do the cooking as well?" Emily had drawn up both her legs and slung her arms around them, her chin resting on her knees. She looked ten years younger than her age in that position.

"You make it sound like a chore." Marianne stood up. "A full house means six guests, and that's a rarity. It's really no trouble."

"Do you have a menu?"

"No." Marianne was surprised at the sudden harshness that had crept into her voice—it rarely happened that guests had that effect on her. She quickly corrected herself. "Do you have any allergies I should know about?" She recognised her reaction, though. But she knew how to be careful.

"None. Thanks." Emily was still looking up at her.

"Dinner in about an hour?"

"Sounds great."

"There's no dress code by the way." She only mentioned it because Emily—even when wet from swimming in the ocean and relaxed with a beer in her hand—looked like the kind of girl who was used to dressing up for dinner.

"Do you need help?"

Marianne wasn't expecting that question.

"Can you cook?" She felt a smile tug at her lips. *The girl is full of surprises.*

"A little. I took some classes back home and a chef with a name so long I can't possibly remember it taught me how to make a mean curry when I was up north."

"If you can chop a vegetable without losing a finger, you're very welcome in my kitchen." Cooking was always such a solitary, meditative time for Marianne, but she didn't mind the intrusion. "I'm just going to freshen up first. Get out of this bikini."

"If you must." Emily winked at her and Marianne felt the blush rise again. She quickly made her way inside and pretended she hadn't heard.

Maybe Emily wasn't the spoiled little brat she had—admittedly—first taken her for. Even so, Marianne made a mental note to make it absolutely clear that her birthday was not an event to be celebrated.

EMILY

Had she been flirting with the Lodge owner? What on earth had possessed her? Emily looked at herself in the mirror in her room. She hardly still resembled the girl who had boarded a plane for Singapore three months ago. Her hair was so long and light in colour. The blue of her eyes popped out against the brown of her skin. She'd always believed that, just like her mother, she had no talent for tanning, but look at her now. Persistence really did help. Not always though. She'd tried long enough with Jasper. She had persisted. It still hadn't worked.

She looked skinnier as well. Maybe even too skinny, although her mother would certainly not agree with that. What would she do when she got back? Take the position at her father's company that had been reserved for her since she was born? She hadn't excelled academically like her two brothers, hadn't breezed through university like everyone else in the family—even her mother in her day, if she was to be believed.

Here she stood, three months older but none the wiser. Maybe a real conversation with a non-judgmental stranger was exactly what she needed. Someone far removed from the situation, but with enough knowledge of social pressure and family ties to understand. Marianne seemed to fit that bill quite perfectly.

And she was younger than her mother—by ten years even. The confirmation hadn't just come from Marianne announcing the number. It was as if Emily had seen her grow younger before her very eyes. Obviously, something had happened in the woman's life. Something devastating enough to chase her out of her home country and make her hate her birthday, but Emily had seen her perk up. She had noticed the laughter lines crinkle around her temples, and she'd been amazed at how Marianne's biceps curved from under the wet sleeve of her t-shirt when she brought the bottle of beer to her mouth.

By god. She had been flirting. What should she wear for dinner? She tore herself away from the mirror and rummaged through her backpack. Every single item of her clothing was either severely wrinkled or plain dirty. She fished out a white tank top that had seen brighter days, but at this stage of her trip, it was the best she could come up with. She finished her casual outfit with a pair of skimpy jean shorts. Not that she was trying to dress to impress. The utter foolishness of it.

Emily found Marianne in the kitchen downstairs. She inadvertently blinked when she walked in. Should women over forty not always wear a bra? Even merely to counter the laws of gravity? Marianne obviously didn't think so. Maybe she was one of those wild chicks her mother sometimes talked about with a wrinkle of disgust curling under her nose. The ones who burned their bra and regarded them as a symbol of female oppression.

"Hey," Marianne greeted her.

She'd been so absorbed with stealing glances at Marianne's chest that she hadn't even taken in the kitchen yet. It looked as if it had been designed by Nigella Lawson herself.

Emily whistled between her teeth. A cat call the old her would never have dared to utter. Then again, this wolf whistle was only aimed at the stainless steel of the kitchen and the pots and pans suspended from hooks along the walls. "Jesus. I'm not a psychologist, but could there be some overcompensation going on here? You know, like middle-aged men with flashy sports cars?"

Marianne looked her over. It was hard for Emily to keep her gaze fixed on her face because the chef's nipples clearly had a life of their own and poked pointedly through the flimsy fabric of the faded The Cure t-shirt she now had on.

"But no chef's whites, huh?" Emily couldn't help herself.

Marianne flushed bright red. A typical British complexion. Emily knew all about that herself and she instantly felt sorry for her host.

"Sorry, I didn't mean to be untoward." The conservatively raised girl in her—the one she'd been trying to escape the grips of on this trip—bubbled to the surface.

"My fault entirely," Marianne said with slightly bowed head. "They're not usually so... disobedient."

They both burst out laughing at the same time. Not just giggles, but loud cackles that served more to release the tension than to mark the comic quality of the situation.

"What's cooking?" Emily asked after the waves of laughter had subsided.

"Pad Thai all right? It's not very original, but I make my own version and it's not too shabby."

"Sounds wonderful. What can I do?"

"If you could chop those, that would be wonderful." Marianne pointed at a bunch of green onions.

They seemed to have been left there for the sole purpose of audience participation as Marianne visibly had everything else under control. She worked quickly and methodically—like the chefs in professional kitchens on TV—and by the time Emily had sliced the onions the kitchen smelled like the essence of Thai food: fiery peppers, garlic and a delicious mix of spices. Emily suddenly felt quite hungry.

For the next twenty minutes she watched Marianne assemble the dish. Almost entranced by her graceful movements around the designer kitchen, Emily hardly noticed Marianne's bra-less state anymore—except when she reached up to grab something from a cabinet above the cooker.

"Dinner's ready," Marianne said, with a smile so bright it stirred something in the pit of Emily's stomach. Or maybe it was just hunger.

MARIANNE

They ate dinner while staring out into the fleeting light of dusk. Marianne loved the time of day—because it was hardly evening yet—when the ocean seemed to disappear and all that remained was the spot she created for herself with candles and discreet lighting.

"It's so quiet here," Emily said. If she was enjoying the food, she hadn't said so yet, which was terribly un-upper class of her. Marianne suppressed a smile at the thought.

"That's why I love it." She chewed on some noodles while contemplating if she should continue, but then didn't hesitate. As if, for some reason on this evening, it needed to be said. "It's the only place where I can find some sort of peace."

Marianne could tell Emily didn't immediately know how to respond to that. She fidgeted with a piece of chicken on her plate and avoided her gaze. When she finally did look up, Marianne was surprised by the intensity in her eyes.

"I gathered as much." She put her fork down. "Hey, I'm running from something too." Emily's voice had gone soft, barely a whisper against the light breeze sweeping in from the sea. "And if you can't be at home, this place isn't half bad."

An opening. Marianne took it. "What are you running from?"

The corners of Emily's mouth curled into a tight smile, as if she'd been waiting for the question and the right time for it to be asked.

"A terribly expensive wedding and a subsequent life I stopped being able to imagine, I guess."

Marianne couldn't hold back a grin at being subjected to more dramatic vagueness. "Did you leave him at the altar?"

"As good as." She reached for her beer. "It broke my heart as much as it did his, you know. But of course no one could see that. He was my best friend for five years, my life really, and I loved him—I still love him, I always will—but as our wedding day approached, an uneasiness kept building inside of me. First, I brushed it off as nerves because I simply couldn't stop lying to myself. I'd been doing it for so long by then. And it was so easy with him." She took a breath before continuing. "But I knew in my heart that it wasn't right to promise eternity when I couldn't even face the next day." Emily fell silent, but Marianne didn't press her. She was starting to put the pieces together and, oddly, despite the sadness creeping into Emily's expression, Marianne grew excited about the words she suspected to hear next.

"All throughout planning the wedding, which was to be a momentous occasion for both of our families, I'd fooled myself into believing that the love I felt was enough. That it was based on a solid, deeply-rooted friendship and what could possibly be more important than that?" She shook her head. "But one day I looked at myself in the mirror and asked my reflection how on earth I had become a twenty-four-year-old who didn't allow herself any passion. I mean, my family's not very big on passion and I've always been taught that getting along well with your partner is so much more valuable and sustainable than that 'short bout of foolishness'—my mother's words—at the beginning of a relationship." Emily's fingers seemed about to strangle the neck of the bottle she was holding. "That's when I realised my idea of love had been wrong all along. And that I didn't want to end up twenty-five years later giving the same advice to my daughter."

She took a long gulp from her beer and some of it ran down her chin. She wiped it off with such a sweet, almost child-like gesture.

"It's like when you make a puzzle and the last pieces just won't fit and you cram them in anyway. As if that's what I'd been doing with my life. Well, one day, they're going to come loose and nothing clicks anymore."

Marianne was amazed by the sudden clarity in Emily's words and by the eloquence she displayed in explaining something so personal and complex. "Wow." She didn't really know if she should speak yet, but the need to acknowledge Emily's confession as something big and valid and true was too great. "That must have taken a lot of courage." Marianne had no trouble picturing Emily's family. She had one just like it of her own.

"It wasn't even courage. It was just... need. An undeniable desire for something else." Emily drew her eyes into slits. Marianne noticed the sparkle of the first tear that gathered in the corner of her eye.

"I mean... I know what I want, I've known all along, really. I just..." She paused. "I just haven't allowed myself to give in to these feelings ever, which is silly and stupid in so many ways, but I always had Jasper and I thought I always had to give it at least one more try..." She wiped away the lone tear running down her cheek. "And I would never have cheated on him, not on anyone."

Poor girl. All of this had been bottled up inside of her for years. For some it was so easy, while others just found it so difficult. Marianne briefly reflected on her own life and how simple love had been before it had become cruel and nearly destroyed her. "Have you ever told anyone about this before?"

Slowly, Emily shook her head. The tears started streaming rapidly now, painting tracks on her cheeks that reflected in the flicker of the candlelight.

Marianne moved out of her chair to give Emily a hug.

EMILY

Embarrassment was not the right word to describe how Emily felt, it was more a mixture of quiet shame for rambling on like that and an enormous sense of relief. Marianne's arms around her only acted as more of a catalyst to let her emotions run free—mostly in the shape of tears raining down her cheeks.

But what was this? Three months of endlessly mulling it over in her head and she still couldn't say it? Was she that afraid of who she really was? Could she even say the word out loud?

"I know I'm a complete outsider on this matter." Marianne's mouth was very close to Emily's ear. "But it sounds to me as if you've made the right decision."

Emily nodded. She knew that much, but that decision was only the beginning. Walking away was hard, but going back and starting anew would be even harder.

"I'm sorry for blubbering like this," she managed to say. "Trust me, I'm not usually like this." She felt a chuckle make its way through Marianne's muscles.

"There's no one here to judge you."

This simple remark from Marianne set loose another round of tears, because that's exactly what it came down to in the end. To be free from any judgement and all the expectations heaped upon her from the day she was born. It was the reason why Emily had hopped on that plane and had flown all those miles.

"I—" she started. "I like…"

Marianne's arms hugged her tighter, as if wanting to squeeze the words out of her.

"I like girls… women, I mean." The words tumbled clumsily out of Emily's mouth. She was on a beach in

Thailand in the company of a woman she barely knew—a kind stranger she had just happened upon—and Emily didn't know what she had expected to occur the instant she finally dared to say it, but the moment could not have felt more right. She'd reached the end point of her journey and soon she'd be ready—really ready—to go home.

"And there's absolutely nothing wrong with that." Marianne's grip on her loosened, her hands snaking to Emily's neck. A ball of fire seemed to come alive underneath Emily's skin, as if, now that she'd finally said it—confessed her secret to a perfect stranger—she was allowed to feel it too.

As if she had no choice at all, she stopped thinking and placed her hand on Marianne's. She snuck her fingers around the woman's palm and held on for dear life—as if her body was convinced she'd never meet anyone as sympathetic as this again.

"It's going to be all right." Marianne briefly dug her fingers into the flesh of Emily's shoulders, sending a jolt of lightning through her body, before retreating. She let her hand slip out of Emily's grasp and kneeled beside her. "Believe me, I've been where you are and I know."

"W-what?" Emily felt her eyes grow wide.

"I received my toaster oven a long time ago."

Emily pinched her eyebrows together and, confused, repeated, "What?"

"Silly inside lesbian joke, never mind." Marianne patted her on the thigh and returned to her seat.

Clearly Emily was not enough of a lesbian yet to get it.

"I've never…" She felt heat rise from her neck to her cheeks. "You know."

"What?" Marianne tilted her head, clearly adamant to not cut Emily any slack with this part of her impromptu confession. "Had a slice of toast before?" Her lips curled into a smile, breaking her face into a kind, gentle expression. The crow's feet around her eyes crinkled beautifully.

Emily smiled back. Marianne's words started to register at last.

"Hey, we've all been there at some point." Marianne broke the silence. A sudden darkness seemed to take hold of her face, her confident smile fading and the sparkle in her eye dying.

Emily racked her brain for something to say. Should she ask? They were sharing, after all.

"Do you want to talk about it?" She kept her voice soft and inviting.

Marianne locked her gaze on Emily, eyes boring deep and face unflinching. Emily swallowed hard and concluded she might be in over her head a bit. This was a sombreness she had yet to encounter in her life. A dull sadness hung in the air and swept away any of the elation Emily had been feeling.

"I'm sorry. I didn't mean to pry." What was she thinking? That because they'd had a short moment of bonding over the fact that they were both gay was going to make this stranger open up to her?

"It's not your fault." Marianne's voice was unrecognisable, coming from a low, desperate place. One where words failed. "I just... can't..." Marianne pushed her chair away from the table. "By no means do I want to trivialise the moment we shared tonight by storming off. I'm genuinely happy for you, but I need to go upstairs now."

She walked to the edge of the yard and closed the gate, her movements sparse and precise. When she walked past the table where Emily sat she remained silent. Only when she'd reached the door to the house, she turned around.

"Just let the door fall into the lock and twist it around twice when you go inside. Goodnight."

The tremble in her voice was unmistakable. And so was the pain etched in the lines of her face.

MARIANNE

Marianne could kick herself for her cold reaction. The girl had just admitted something life-changing to herself—and to Marianne. Something Marianne could relate to like no other, no less, and this was how she responded? Slinking off like a thief in the night as if it could ever undo the past? As if it made a difference?

Any sliver of joy, any indication that she might enjoy herself a bit too much, and the guilt set in. Like the storm clouds in rainy season, drenching a perfectly good day in a million tears. And all there was to show for them afterwards were a few puddles that dried up in a matter of hours.

But she was guilty. And instead of doing time in a prison cell, she spent it in paradise. In perpetual exile, because no one could punish her better than she could herself. When people arrived here, on her little patch of land on Samui, they only saw the palm trees, the glittering ocean and white-headed waves, but they didn't see—couldn't see—what wasn't there. The missing person. Nothing could be more punishment for Marianne than spending her days here, in this place that people dream of, without Ingrid.

She peeled off her clothes and slipped into bed. It would have to be a night of medicated sleep. She hadn't had one of those for a while, had somehow managed to keep the demons at bay—some days it was easier than others, but more so of late. She grabbed a strip of pills from the nightstand—always close by—and swallowed one dry. Sleep came within minutes.

"Toast?" Marianne grinned broadly—overcompensating for last night's insensitivity, no doubt. And yes, she'd had a one-way heart-to-heart with Emily, but that didn't make her qualified to predict her sense of humour, especially before breakfast. Even though it was almost ten. Gosh, the girl slept late. Marianne had been up for hours, skulking around the house, hushing herself when she made too much noise.

"Do I get my own toaster now?" Emily still looked a bit groggy, a pinch of moon dust had gathered in the corner of her right eye, but she was awake enough for a quip. Clearly, she hadn't showered yet. Marianne would have heard—but even if she hadn't—the crumpled look of Emily's clothes and the riot that was her hair gave that away.

Suddenly, without notice and from the far recesses of her brain, Marianne envisioned herself waking up to the very sight before her eyes, to a warm body next to hers.

She blinked twice rapidly and shook off the thought. *Where on earth did that come from?*

"I'll call HQ and see what I can do." Marianne found herself rummaging around the kitchen, looking for things she didn't need. "Coffee or tea?"

"Strong coffee, please." Emily rubbed her temples ostentatiously. "After you went to bed, I helped myself to some more beer from the fridge. I hope that's all right. I lined up the bottles so you could count them and charge me."

Marianne had indeed found three empty Singha bottles in the kitchen this morning. She'd cleared them without giving them any further thought. "Nonsense. This is an all-inclusive lesbian resort, you know."

"But—" Marianne could see Emily struggling to get past her utter Britishness and say something about money. "I want to pay. It's only fair."

"Why don't you sit down outside and I'll bring your breakfast out in a second."

"As you wish," Emily shrugged and headed towards the patio, which was drenched in sunlight. Marianne watched her for a second and saw her stretch like a cat, her long arms leaning over the back of the chair, seemingly reaching towards her. For some reason, Marianne felt inclined to meet them and take Emily's hands in hers.

"I'll leave you in peace," Marianne, suddenly feeling defensive, said, when she brought Emily her coffee and toast with little jam and butter cups.

"Please stay, if you don't have anything else to do." Emily's eyes were bright and blue, catching the sunlight. "I, huh, like talking to you."

"I'll be right back." Marianne giggled inwardly as she sauntered to the kitchen to fetch herself a mug of coffee. When she dragged a chair back from the table at which Emily sat munching toast a few minutes later, it couldn't have felt more right. She wanted to stretch out her body as well, the way cats do after a satisfying nap. Instead, she faced Emily with a straight back. Some things can never be unlearned no matter how far you remove yourself from the place you were taught.

"Thank you for last night," Emily said in between bites, almost casually. There was something different about her today, a lighter air, as if a weight had been lifted. Although Marianne had no objective way of measuring this, since she'd only just met her and only had half a day to go on. But she could well imagine how Emily was feeling. "You've no idea how much I needed to say those words."

"I'm glad I was witness to them." Marianne did in no way underestimate the power of the moment for Emily.

"Do you mind me asking what it was like for you?" Emily seemed much bolder today, like someone who had for the first time truly realised the splendour of the life she had to live.

But Marianne had no intention of sharing. Even if she wanted to, she couldn't. It was not part of the deal she'd made with herself five years ago. It was not part of the punishment. She wasn't here for sharing, nor for revelling in past, very fleeting, but profoundly impacting moments of happiness. She was here for penance and penance only.

"Maybe later." She found herself unable to close the door on Emily and the conversation completely though. That was a first.

EMILY

"I'm sorry if I was too forward last night. I'm usually not, but what with my big revelation and all. I didn't quite feel like myself." Marianne wore a faded black Velvet Underground t-shirt today. She must have a vast collection. Emily firmly believed her host didn't dress like that back in Britain. That it was as much a defence mechanism and escape from whatever had happened as her exile here. She wouldn't press Marianne for more information, of course—that would obviously never work—but she could gently probe.

"Or maybe you did." Marianne looked at her over the rim of her cup. She really was an expert at fending off questions. "What's on your agenda today?"

"Some time by the pool, on the beach and with my nose in a book." She smiled at the prospect. "Busy times. Love it."

"Excellent choices." Marianne put her cup down. "And just so you know, there are a few good restaurants along the beach and I can arrange for transportation if you want to go into town."

"Thanks. I may venture a few steps to the left or the right, but most part of the day will be spent on my backside in this truly lovely spot."

"If you do decide to venture out, the squid three doors down is to die for."

"Well, I wouldn't go that far…" Emily grinned stupidly at Marianne. "What does your day look like?" She couldn't remember ever having asked any other of the hotel owners or staff where she'd stayed at. Then again, she'd never come out to any of them on her first night there, either.

"A couple of guests are arriving at noon."

Emily noticed the spark of disappointment taking root in her stomach at hearing this news. As if she somehow regretted that she wouldn't have Marianne, and her lovely house, all to herself anymore. How selfish.

"So I'll be here throughout the day." Marianne winked and it caught Emily so off guard she nearly choked on her last piece of toast. "In case you need me."

"That's good to know," she managed. And it really was good to know.

Emily lounged by the pool the rest of the morning. In any other place, she would have plugged in her headphones and escaped the intruding sounds of her surroundings, but here she took comfort in hearing Marianne scurrying about, talking to the woman who came in to help her and showing the new guests around.

"Dao's making club sandwiches for the new arrivals," Marianne's voice, out of nowhere, beamed behind Emily a bit past noon. "Want one?" Emily had been ignoring the rumbling sounds of her stomach, eager to stay as motionless as possible in the heat.

"I think I'll go try that squid you mentioned earlier." Emily watched Marianne ponder her response.

"Excellent idea."

Emily didn't reply, as if waiting for Marianne to continue… or perhaps offer to join. Another pang of disappointment rushed through her at Marianne's matter-of-factness.

"You may want to put on some more sunscreen when you walk along the beach. Enjoy and see you later." She turned on her heels and focused her attention on the other guests. An older couple with, if Emily had heard correctly, a rather thick Scottish accent.

Feeling somehow stood up—although she couldn't exactly pinpoint why—Emily had no other choice but to gather her affairs and find the beachside seafood restaurant on her own.

Restaurant was a big word for the shack-like structure that displayed its freshly caught wares in a kayak filled with ice under the shade of a palm tree right on the beach. The food was succulent though, and the view breathtaking. Emily stuffed herself with squid grilled with pepper and garlic, so simple but so heavenly, spicy Thai soup and a huge plate of morning glory.

She'd been eating most of her meals alone for weeks on end, but now, all of a sudden, it grated. Some people's company was so much superior to other's. She made her way back to The Red Lodge, which was not, as the name would suggest, painted red on the outside. In fact, the colour red was quite absent for an establishment boasting it in its name. She'd have to ask Marianne about that. Maybe she would even reply.

To her disappointment, she didn't immediately spot Marianne upon her return. There was no sign of the Scottish couple either and the Lodge seemed suddenly too deserted. Maybe Emily had reached her threshold of being alone. Last night, her trip had reached its conclusion when she'd finally said the words to someone. Words so obvious, but somehow so difficult to utter. Until she met Marianne.

She dumped her bag on a patio chair, extracted the sunscreen and applied a fresh coat before tip-toeing through the hot sand to the shore line. After a refreshing dive into the lazy waves, she turned her back to the horizon and squinted in the direction of the seemingly empty Lodge. The water was indigo, the sand pearly white. *What a place to come out of the closet.* But, of course, she knew it was only the beginning. The real work still lay ahead. Braving the disappointment in her mother's gaze. She could perfectly predict Jasper's flabbergasted reaction as she was sure he didn't have a clue. And was her father ready to employ a lesbian solicitor at his firm?

Emily dipped her head back under water—not too long as not to miss Marianne's return to the Lodge—and revelled in the fact that she had a few more days of peace and quiet before returning to real life.

MARIANNE

Despite promising Emily she'd be around all day, Marianne found herself fleeing the Lodge—her self-created safe haven. For some reason, it didn't feel so safe anymore. Marianne had faced numerous probing questions before and had always shrugged them off elegantly, with a quip and a chuckle, quickly and efficiently. Her usual modus operandi didn't seem to work with Emily. The most disconcerting aspect of it was that it wasn't because of Emily's gentle insistence—nothing she hadn't dealt with before—but because of that melting feeling beneath her stomach.

"Another one please, Sam." She tapped a finger against the sweaty neck of her beer bottle.

"You're killing them off fast today." He looked at his worn watch ostentatiously. "Bit early, even for a die-hard lesbian like yourself."

Not in the mood for banter, Marianne didn't take the bait. She shot her friend a crooked smile and he knew her well enough to leave it alone. Sometimes, when the silence inside her head became too deafening, Marianne did visit Sam's bar for a bout of meaningless conversation. When she hadn't had guests in a while and even the Lodge, with its sprawling view, felt too isolated. Today, though, her mind was not quiet but busy trying to figure out why Emily's presence had such an instant effect on her.

Sam planted another beer in front of her and, with a wink, retreated to the other side of the bar. A group of three backpackers sat by the open window, but Marianne easily blocked out the noise they made.

She brought the bottle to her mouth, letting the cold liquid cool her off from the inside.

Marianne definitely recognised herself in Emily. The posh background. The doubts. The relief of telling someone. The crushing social expectations. In the end, it all hadn't really mattered. It had all worked itself out, until that day…

She saw a version of herself in Emily she hadn't been acquainted with for so long. That eager look in her blue eyes, speaking of a life not free of challenges but wide open with possibility. Sentiments unimaginable to Marianne now. Seeing such desire for life burn in Emily's eyes made her look back, though. It made her remember a time she didn't allow herself, out of sheer self-preservation, to revisit.

It also made her feel something she hadn't felt in years. A crack in her guard she'd worked so hard to keep up—she'd deemed absolutely necessary for her own survival. Emily's innocence and unassuming way of asking questions almost made her want to answer them.

Maybe it was time. Maybe the wall had been up long enough for the most broken pieces of her to heal behind it.

Not before she had another beer, though. She signalled Sam, who was busy washing glasses at the sink.

"Either you tell me what's going on," Sam said as he deposited a glass of ice water in front of her, "or I ban you from my bar. And I damn well know this is your favourite place on the island." The grin that came with his statement was disarming, his thick Australian accent charming as always.

Marianne shoved the water aside. "Give me another beer and I may well tell you all my best kept secrets."

"I'm not asking for your secrets, darling." Sam leaned onto the counter of the bar with his elbows. "But it's not like you to come here in the middle of the afternoon and get hammered."

"There's this girl," Marianne blurted out. She shook her head before continuing, feeling as if she'd already said too much. Emily was just a girl passing through, like so many others. There was no reason why she should be any different.

"Ah." Sam's knuckle briefly touched her wrist. "About time."

Marianne knew he meant well, but his response was enough to snap her out of it. She'd left the Lodge after watching Emily trail off to the fish restaurant and had skipped lunch altogether. Her head was spinning from too much beer, her guard was slipping and she needed to be alone. Sleep it off. Make it go away. Again.

"I'd better go." She reached for the pocket of her jeans shorts. "What's the score?"

"Pay me later." Sam grabbed her by the arm. "And give me your car keys, please. I'll call Aran and have him take you home."

Marianne had never told Sam about what had driven her to seek solitary refuge in Thailand and he had no way of knowing that his words would rouse such emotion from her. Marianne fought hard against the tears. Unable to fend them off on her own, she reached for the glass of water and swallowed a few icy gulps. They left her cold inside, just the way she liked it.

She waited for Aran in silence, a fatigue creeping through her flesh. She just wanted to sleep. And forget. Maybe even pretend Emily wasn't here so she didn't have to experience these feelings. What were they anyway? Hormones?

After Aran dropped her off, she went straight up the stairs, avoiding any possible contact with Emily or the other guests. She drew the curtains shut and pretended it was long after night fall. She fell onto her bed, fully clothed, screwed her eyes shut and tried to convince herself everything could stay the same until she fell asleep. She woke up just before ten p.m.

EMILY

Emily spent the rest of the afternoon alone, wondering where Marianne had gone. After nibbling on a pomelo salad while engaged in reluctant conversation with the Scots—she'd much rather be talking to Marianne over dinner—she fetched her Kindle and retreated to the beach with a beer.

Her eyes kept drifting away from the illuminated screen, off into the black horizon in front of her, while her thoughts always came back to Marianne. Why was she so secretive? Although Emily was quite certain Marianne would just call it discreet. What had brought her here? If Emily really wanted to, she could find out. Few people leave Holland Park behind for Koh Samui, and her father would quite possibly know about it. But this would require sending him an e-mail and establishing contact with home a few days too soon. She needed the time between now and going home to sort some things out in her head.

Also, if Marianne wanted her to know anything at all, it was up to her to tell Emily.

"Any good?"

The voice behind her startled her. She'd been so wrapped up in her thoughts she hadn't heard Marianne's footsteps approach. Instantly, a tension that had nestled into her muscles over the course of the day—a day spent looking out for Marianne—fell away from her.

"They always make these female detectives so strong and independent and hot… and straight. It frustrates me."

Marianne looked a bit worse for wear, as if she'd just finished a night shift somewhere. Her hair stood up on one side, her eyes drooped and sported black circles underneath them. That was all Emily could make out in the dark. But it was good to see her at last.

"You'd best get used to that." Marianne chuckled and crouched next to her. "I'm sorry for disappearing on you today," she whispered.

Silence hung between them for a few seconds.

"I'm sure you had a good reason for that." Saying it caused Emily to re-evaluate her expectations. Why had her eyes been busy searching for the slightest sign of Marianne all day? Surely, she'd spent the rest of her holiday trying to avoid other people.

"If you call getting wasted on cheap beer in the middle of the afternoon a good reason, then sure." Marianne shifted her weight and let her behind drop into the sand.

"You're free to do as you please. That's the whole point, right?" Emily glanced at Marianne who stared out into the ink black night. The skin of her cheek closest to Emily was a bit wrinkled. She just nodded absent-mindedly.

"Night swim?" Marianne asked after a while. She turned her head to face Emily and her eyes burned through the blackness of the night.

Emily was on her feet in a split second. She was still wearing her bathers underneath her shorts and tank top and she rushed them off her in record time. "Yes, please." She watched Marianne hesitate. Her eyes stopped at Marianne's t-shirt and she immediately understood. She suppressed a grin and said, "Race you."

"Hey, that's not fair—" Marianne's words were drowned out by the slapping roar of the waves.

Emily waded into the water and looked back. She witnessed Marianne struggle out of her shorts before walking towards her in a pair of white panties and her t-shirt. *Should be interesting when wet.*

"Forgot something?" Emily asked when Marianne faced her in the water.

"As usual." Marianne grinned, her eyes glinting in the moonlight. It was a half-smile that seemed to connect with Emily's stomach, leaving it feeling funny. Then there was that warm, fuzzy sensation making its way through her blood. And the sudden need for swim goggles so she could dive under and sneak a peek.

Apart from the faint sound of voices drifting towards them from one of the nearby resorts, everything was quiet around them. It was a stillness Emily was not used to, or maybe it was the child in her, and she started splashing Marianne with water. Gently at first, but her enthusiasm—and her lack of knowing what to say or do, quickly took over and soon she was dousing Marianne in handfuls of salty sea water.

"Hey," Marianne shrieked. "I always give as good as I get." She moved her arms through the water and over her head, her wet t-shirt clinging to her skin, and it was almost enough to make Emily stop in her tracks, but she couldn't stop now. It would be a bit too obvious.

Water hit Emily straight in the face and while she was still busy trying to spit it out, she felt a pair of hands grab her below the knee and pull her under.

When she came back up for air, Marianne stared her in the face triumphantly. "That should teach you not to mess with me." She stood tall in the water, only covered to the middle of her thighs, and Emily couldn't keep her eyes off the water drops cascading down the other woman's skin-tight, soaked clothes.

"I surrender," she managed to squeeze out of her throat as a desire quite new to her swept through her flesh.

And if it was an invitation on Marianne's part to instigate something, or even ask an inquisitive question, Emily missed that entirely because her body had become the master of her mind. She witnessed how Marianne's hard nipples poked through the drenched fabric of her t-shirt and all she could think was how lucky she was to be under water so Marianne wouldn't notice how soaked her bikini bottoms were.

MARIANNE

Marianne wondered if she was still drunk, the way she stood there in her wet attire facing Emily, who clearly was beyond words at the sight of her. The utter inappropriateness of the situation hit her like a fist in the gut. And she really should start wearing a bra more often.

She could barely make out the blue of Emily's eyes in the darkness, but when their gazes met over the black surface of the water, and for some reason Marianne's breath caught in her throat, she slowly started walking back to shore.

"I'll fetch us some towels." She turned away from Emily, afraid to look back and witness the raw emotions laid bare in Emily's stare. The water was heavy against her legs, but she was practically running out of the ocean, having no clue how to deal with the rising fire in her blood.

Marianne waited long enough by the stack of fluffy towels to make sure the moment had passed before returning to the beach. Her hands were shaking a little too much for her comfort when she offered Emily the towel because all she really wanted to do was wrap it around her and pull her close like she had done the night before.

Maybe she shouldn't have done that.

"Thanks," Emily murmured. Drops of water slid off her onto the sand and Marianne couldn't help herself. She caught a good look before Emily covered most of her skin with the towel.

"I guess you've had enough beer for one day?" Emily asked while shifting her weight from one foot to the other, her voice thin and tight.

"I—" She hesitated. It took more will power than Marianne had expected to reply in a sensible manner. "I'll have some water."

She made her way through the garden, hurrying to the kitchen, unable to tear herself away from Emily for the rest of night.

They sat down in the sand, enveloped in the almost-silence of the beach—just the gentle slapping of waves and the smacking of their lips as they drank.

Marianne knew small talk would not do. But how do you open a box that hasn't been opened for years, a locked box of which the key went missing a long time ago? She couldn't possibly share her burden with someone so young. It wasn't fair. Still, the simple fact that she sat next to another woman merely contemplating the option made a shiver run up her spine.

Maybe thaw was setting in.

"I know, huh…" Emily started. "I know we haven't talked much and we only just met, but I feel so at ease around you. Like I've known you forever."

Marianne had to swallow the lump in her throat before she could reply. "We come from the same stock, I guess." Her voice trembled. "Upper crust London." She quickly pushed away the thought of her father's last five messages on her phone that had gone unanswered. "Both gay. Both running."

"Do you..." Emily hesitated again and Marianne felt like such a coward for making a twenty-four-year-old do all the heavy lifting in this late night conversation. "I guess I'm wondering if you feel it too."

They both stared ahead. A few stars twinkled above the sea.

"What I feel doesn't matter." A cold hand wrapped itself around Marianne's heart. Emily turned to her. Marianne didn't move despite being able to see, from the corner of her eye, the desperate expression conquering Emily's face.

"Why?" Emily asked.

"Because it's the only way I know how to survive." Emily had no idea what sitting on the beach with her after sunset and simply saying those words—no matter their bluntness—took out of Marianne. To Marianne, it presented another crack in her well-crafted armour. She swivelled around in the sand and somehow found the courage—because how could she not?—to face the girl. "But if you really must know." Marianne realised her words were barely audible over the crashing of the waves. "Yes, I do."

Emily cleared her throat before speaking. "It may not matter to you, but what you feel matters to me."

The tears stinging behind her eyes were exactly the reason why Marianne didn't have conversations like this anymore. This one was about to end abruptly either way, because Marianne didn't have words left. She fought the animalistic impulse inside of her to lean forward and kiss Emily. Instead, she briefly reached for Emily's palm and squeezed it gently before pushing herself up out of the sand. "Thanks," she muttered quietly, turned around and walked inside.

When she arrived in her room, she sat down on the bed, buried her face in her hands and let the tears roll out.

It had happened once before. A sudden instant of standing face-to-face with a stranger that had changed her life. And look at the pain that had caused.

Marianne didn't reach for a sleeping pill that night. Instead, before stripping off her wet clothes and going to bed, she walked to the window facing the ocean and looked for Emily. She could just make out her hunched shape at the edge of the garden—more a shadow really. As much as she tried, she couldn't look away. Not this time.

EMILY

A knock on her bedroom door woke Emily from the lazy slumber she'd been indulging in for the past hour.

"Emily?" The sound of Marianne's voice had the same shock effect as a bucket of cold water being poured over her sleepy head. "Are you awake?"

"Yes. Just a second," Emily groaned while scanning the room for a piece of clothing to cover herself with. Last night's towel was the first thing she found. She quickly folded it around her naked body and padded to the door to open it.

"Morning." The unexpectedly bright smile Marianne greeted her with nearly floored her. "I'm sorry for disturbing you but it's almost eleven and I just wanted to see if you were all right."

"I'm fine." Emily suppressed a grin at the sight of Marianne's AC/DC t-shirt, and the obvious absence of a bra beneath it. "Do you check on all your guests?"

The lines around Marianne's eyes crinkled up. "No. Just you." She fiddled with her fingers before continuing. "Just so you don't think I'm disappearing on you again, I'm meeting someone for lunch in town today, but I'll be back after in case… erm, you want to talk or grab a beer together."

Emily couldn't hide the smile splitting her face. "Thanks for letting me know."

"Sure." Marianne lingered by the door a bit longer, as if wanting to say something else. "See you later." She turned on her heels and sauntered off. Emily's eyes followed her as Marianne crossed through the hallway and climbed the stairs. The same sensation that had stirred her blood in the ocean the night before descended upon her. Only, this time she wasn't wearing any clothes underneath the towel and she could swear the throbbing between her legs vibrated throughout her body.

She quickly shut the door and headed for the shower.

After getting dressed, Emily decided to forego a late breakfast at the Lodge and returned to the fish restaurant where she had lunch the day before.

While munching on more squid, kale with garlic and a spicy chicken dish—way too much for someone eating alone—she overlooked the ocean and wondered what it was like to cut yourself off from everything and everyone you once knew for years. She'd attempted to do the same the past three months, but she'd always been more or less in contact with someone from the hometront. She'd always been slated to go back. And her heart had opened itself to someone new much sooner than she'd anticipated after breaking off the engagement to Jasper.

She certainly hadn't embarked on her solitary adventure to experience a holiday romance. She'd come to think things through. To evaluate. To finally be able to say the words. To confirm that she'd made the right decision. Her mission was complete. She had been ready to go back and then… Marianne had entered the scene.

Marianne with the dark eyes and the equally dark past. Curiosity burned inside of her, but Emily knew she shouldn't pry. Especially not now that Marianne had given her the smallest of openings.

She paid a ridiculously small amount for the food and walked back along the shore line—where the sand was wet and cool—to the Lodge.

Emily found Marianne immersed in a book when she returned to the patch of beach on the backside of the lodge. Upon closer inspection, as she approached, she spotted the words *Best Lesbian Erotica* on the cover, which put her at an immediate loss for words.

"Hey." Marianne held one finger between the pages, but closed the book so the cover was now clearly in view. Emily couldn't keep her eyes off the image of the two naked women, albeit quite blurred, in an intimate position on the cover.

"I have more of these, if you're interested." Marianne took off her sunglasses and looked from the book to Emily, her eyes squinting against the sun. "I have a small library upstairs. Come have a browse later."

She can't talk about her troubled past, but she has no problem reading erotica in plain sight? How odd. It wasn't the only thought crowding Emily's brain though. She was intrigued and curious. Because, of course she'd used the internet and her imagination, but she never really had…

"Maybe I will," she mustered, and quickly made her way inside before the blush spreading across her cheeks became too visible.

MARIANNE

Marianne had done it on purpose. She'd sat there waiting for Emily's return to gauge her reaction to her choice of literature, and, by the look of things, it hadn't missed its effect. She hadn't just innocently leafed through the book though, that was quite impossible with the kind of stories it contained, and it had left her in a mild state of arousal. *That had been a while.* She hadn't reached for one of the books in the series for a long time, and the thought of grabbing one to provoke Emily had just popped into her mind. Normally, she wouldn't have allowed herself a silly indulgence like that, but it was as if the whole situation with Emily asked for it. Which was nonsense, of course. Clear and utter nonsense.

While she was there, with the goods in hand, she might as well finish reading the story she'd been engrossed in, despite keeping an eye out for Emily. It was an excellent one, about a woman being seduced by a wine shop owner in Southern Italy. But that was where the similarities ended.

With a pair of drenched bikini bottoms that hadn't been so wet without touching water in some time, Marianne made her way to her bedroom upstairs. She hoped no one would disturb her on the way, because she had some urgent business to attend to.

She didn't lock her door because she never did, she was on the top floor for a reason, and without thinking or hesitation, slipped out of her bathing suit and spread out on the bed. She held on to the images the story had planted in her mind. The shop owner lifting up the visitor's dress and letting her hands roam over her body briefly before slipping them inside of her.

Marianne found her clit rock hard and, to her great surprise, she came quickly and with deep shudders of her muscles after a few quick strokes. The last image she saw in her mind's eye before her body surrendered was one of Emily. It was more a memory, really, of Emily wading into the water that first afternoon by the ocean. It shocked Marianne because she had believed the moment hadn't touched her in the slightest. Quite a few things had changed since then, even though it had happened less than forty-eight hours ago. *Careful Marianne.* But, by god, she had enjoyed the sensation.

A soft knock on the door startled her.

"Marianne?" Emily's voice came from the other side. "Are you there?"

Marianne hurried off the bed looking for something to cover herself with. The easiest option seemed a bathrobe that hung off a hook on the back of the door.

"Just a second." She pulled the cord extra tight around her waist before opening the door. "Yes?"

"Am I disturbing you?"

Marianne didn't pull the door too wide, so as not to expose the evidence of her arousal that she had casually discarded on the floor. "I was just changing." She cleared her throat. Was that a small smile playing on Emily's lips? "How can I help you?"

"I just thought I'd take you up on your offer of visiting your library." The innocence in Emily's tone betrayed that she was anything but innocent.

"I wasn't expecting you so quickly." Marianne decided to give as good as she got. "You must be really curious."

"There's no time like the present, as they say."

What had happened? Why did everything seem so different all of a sudden? So miles away from just yesterday morning. And how did she end up flirting rather shamelessly with a twenty-something at the top of the stairs?

"Would it be all right with you if I put some clothes on first? Just go through there." She pointed in the direction of the door next to her bedroom.

"Why ever would it not be?" Emily said coquettishly before dragging her gaze away from Marianne.

Marianne closed the door and took a few deep breaths. Well, she had started it. The real question was if she could finish it. She pondered wearing a bra for a split second, but, as usual, decided against it. She located her t-shirt and shorts and put them on while her heart thundered furiously beneath her chest.

When she checked herself in the mirror, more out of habit than self-consciousness, her glance fell on the picture of her and Ingrid next to it and, as though the image cast a spell on Marianne, the pitter-patter beneath her ribs grew quieter. Marianne smiled at the golden-framed image—she could do that now, sometimes—and, as if agreeing on something with her former lover beyond time and space, nodded briefly.

Maybe five years *had* been long enough.

"What exactly are you looking for?" Marianne didn't have to put the playfulness in her voice, it was there, showing up uninvitedly but welcome nonetheless.

"Gosh, you really do have quite the collection here." Emily's eyes scanned the rows of books feverishly, like a kid in a candy store. For the very first time. With unlimited funds.

"I would have dusted them off if you'd given me the time."

EMILY

Emily had seen through Marianne's charade. She might be young and maybe even slightly naive, but she wasn't stupid.

She'd spotted Marianne rushing up the stairs, and she'd easily guessed at the reason for her hastiness. It had amused, but also thoroughly aroused her. Maybe more than she'd ever been. Because of the setting and the circumstances, no doubt, but also because of the small signs of a willingness to open up Marianne had started to display.

There she stood. Rising to the challenge, with her nipples stabbing the fabric of her bikini and her clit a throbbing mess in her swim suit. And maybe she could tell herself it was because of the explicit covers of the books she was browsing, but she knew better. It had everything to do with the woman behind her whose body heat she could feel radiate onto her back.

As appealing as some of the books looked, Emily's interest soon wavered. Just as they'd been a ploy for Marianne, they'd been one for her. But, seeing as she didn't really have a clue as to how to proceed, she played the game a while longer.

"The one you were reading seemed rather good." She turned to face Marianne. "Seemed to have a certain urgency to it."

"You're very observant." Marianne took a step in her direction. The room wasn't very big as every wall was covered with book cases.

"So I've been told." The words seemed to roll out of Emily's mouth as swiftly as the breath out of her lungs. Was this what desire really felt like? This swooping rush of want that knocked the wind out of her?

Something changed in Marianne's face then, as though she suddenly recognised the gravity of the situation.

Emily backed up against the book shelves, the wood prodding her ribcage. Not because she was afraid or hesitant, but because she wanted to lengthen the moment in which Marianne came for her. She never wanted to forget the look on her face, the mixture of need, caution, and relief.

"You don't strike me as having doubts about this, but I need to ask, okay?" Marianne's voice had dropped a register or two. "Are you sure?"

Emily bit her lip and nodded. She lifted her hands to Marianne's arms and pulled her close. "God yes," she whispered before pressing her lips against Marianne's.

Instantly, she was lost in the softness of kissing another woman. The utter unexpectedness of it, and the way a simple kiss seemed to change something inside of her, settling in the pit of her stomach and sizzling in her blood.

The kiss grew from tentative to intense rapidly and Emily felt Marianne's body crash against her, forcing her ribs to push harder against the shelves. How fitting, she thought, considering the content of the books behind her.

And how glorious it was to feel a woman's breasts rub against hers, to feel her nipples perk up against her flesh. The softness of Marianne's tongue was unlike anything else she'd ever felt. She had tried to imagine it, of course, but her imagination, as it turned out, had been sorely lacking.

Marianne's tongue swirled inside of Emily's mouth with a passion and urgency she had rarely come across in her life. As if she sensed she was getting too lost in the kiss, Marianne pulled back slightly, ending it with a tender peck.

"Good god," she exhaled more than said. "I, uh, I'm not sure…"

Emily could feel her drift off into that dark space she'd slipped off to last night and, as if it was the only antidote, placed her hands on Marianne's neck and drew her near.

"Please." Emily looked straight into her eyes. "Don't run." She had to swallow. "Stay."

And she did. Marianne's expression softened, the doubts quickly evaporating from her face, and leaned back in for a kiss.

It went deeper this time, at least it touched Emily in a deeper place. Because whatever Marianne was battling through and the significance this kiss held for her, this wasn't a minor moment for Emily either.

Every dip of Marianne's tongue inside her mouth carried Emily further away from the life she once knew. She'd always known there was no way back, but now she clearly felt it as well. Amongst other things. Like a flood of liquid releasing between her legs. And a flock of butterflies swarming through her veins.

"I want you," she whispered in between kisses. She didn't know whether she'd really said it or if Marianne had heard it, but they kept on kissing, kept on exploring each other's mouths with a tenderness that tore down every wall Emily had ever built around herself, and Emily knew she'd never spoken truer words in her life.

"Me too," Marianne whispered back eventually, her hands in Emily's hair. "But it's complicated. I'm complicated. I have a past and—"

"It doesn't matter. None of it matters." And as she said it, as the words left her mouth in a frenzy of lust and desire, she knew she'd asked for too much too soon.

Marianne withdrew almost instantly. "You don't know me, Emily. You don't know anything about me." There was a tremor in her voice and her hands shook.

"Then tell me what I need to know."

MARIANNE

Marianne stared at Emily. Her brain resisted, but every cell in her body begged for mercy, at last. She couldn't just throw herself at Emily, though. That had never been her style and it wouldn't be now, either.

"Let's talk." She tried to keep her voice steady, but failed miserably. "Tonight. Let's have dinner."

"You mean a date?"

Marianne shuddered at the word. "If you will, yes, a date." She indulged Emily.

"Can't wait." Emily made a play for her, tried to catch Marianne's wrist in her hand, but, more on instinct than anything else, Marianne recoiled. She regretted it immediately, but Emily had no idea. Not something Marianne could blame her for, but maybe she should protect her. Maybe her first time shouldn't be with someone like Marianne. Maybe Marianne shouldn't be so selfish and project all of her repressed desires and years of denied lust on this girl who was merely on holiday, merely passing through, which, truth be told, made her appear even more attractive.

She could already see the hurt in Emily's eyes as she withdrew.

"Whatever it is," Emily approached her despite Marianne's reticence, "you think you are, I don't care about your past. I care about the present, about this moment between us, the simple beauty of it. Please, just try to acknowledge that." Emily suddenly seemed wise beyond her years.

"I promise to try." Marianne allowed Emily to touch her again. "I do." She pulled Emily close, her fingers disappearing in the wild locks of her hair, and kissed her again. But to Marianne, it was so much more than a kiss. It was a release from the prison of her mind. An escape from years of torment.

Liquid heat tumbled through her flesh, scorching her bones. She had to restrain herself to not drag Emily to the floor with her and let go of everything there and then. But, unlike that night more than five years ago, Marianne had learned to always let common sense prevail.

It was hard to resist the raw need, the blazing urgency of desire in Emily's eyes when they came up for air and locked gazes, but apart from the fact that it was too much too soon, Marianne had a guest house to run. Thank god for that, she thought, for the umpteenth time in her second life.

"I'll cook for you," she said, trying to bring them back to solid ground. "The other guests have made arrangements to go into town."

Emily nodded and it looked as if it was all she could muster.

"I have some errands to run, but Dao is here if you need anything." Marianne painted on a smile. "Meanwhile, you can borrow any book you like." She slanted her head and pecked Emily on the nose before stepping away.

Emily stood there immobile for a while, eyes wide and panting, and another rush of lust swept through Marianne at the sight of her. *The shackles are off. God help me.* She left the room quickly because she needed to breathe in a different sort of air.

Back in her bedroom, with the door closed behind her, she crumpled down on the bed and didn't fight back the tears. They landed in greedy gulps on her cheeks and knees and arms and they felt as much like freedom as the touch of Emily's tongue against her lips.

She'd promised Emily some sort of explanation and whereas that burden would have been too much—*was* too much—yesterday, today she felt stronger, maybe even ready.

Not that the voice in the back of her mind had completely relinquished control. It was still there, warning not to get in too deep, but really, there wasn't too much danger of that. Emily would be leaving in a few days, and, as cruel as it may have been, Marianne believed that to be an acceptable arrangement. She'd never had a step-by-step approach because she never had a plan except to get away from the events that changed everything about her life, as far as possible, but now that this opportunity presented itself, she knew she had to take it. And, in a way, it was helpful to know that, no matter what happened, a certain boundary simply could not be crossed. It was a precaution Marianne desperately needed.

She took off her clothes, looked at her short black bob in the mirror, the brown of her eyes and the flecks of yellow in them, the swell of her biceps and the squareness of her shoulder line, and, uncharacteristically, thought, why the hell not, before heading for the shower in the en-suite bathroom.

EMILY

Emily had acted on instinct as much as on desire and she had no way of knowing that, a mere half hour after following Marianne up the stairs, she'd stand trembling with her back against a bunch of lesbian erotica anthologies. She turned around and browsed them again, but they couldn't hold her interest anymore. She didn't want words, least of all sentences on paper—no matter how arousing. She wanted action, soft hands on her breasts and nipples in her mouth.

She made her way down and headed straight into the ocean, in desperate need of cooling off. Time went by excruciatingly slowly, as if slowing down to torment her. She couldn't focus on her book, didn't find any songs she wanted to listen to on her iPod, and when Dao served her a drink on the patio, it felt odd to not receive it from Marianne.

She watched the other couple leave and exhaled, hoping they wouldn't return too soon. She waited in vain for a glimpse of Marianne, but either she took her sweet time with the errands or she was actively avoiding Emily until their 'date'. Maybe she had pushed it by calling it that. But maybe Marianne needed a little push. Maybe it was all she needed.

Just as Emily headed to her room to get ready, Marianne walked in.

"Dinner in an hour?" she asked dryly, almost matter-of-factly, as if nothing had changed since she'd asked the same question two nights ago.

Emily nodded and wondered what on earth she'd do with herself the next hour. She opted for a quick shower and a stroll on the beach to at least make an attempt at clearing her head. The problem was that she had no desire to forget about anything that had happened since she arrived.

Marianne served a simple cold beef salad, which tasted delicious enough, but Emily experienced some trouble with her appetite. The moment Marianne had sat down opposite her, hunger had ceased to be of any importance in Emily's world.

Instead of the black t-shirts Emily had only seen her in, Marianne wore a tight sleeveless blouse and the sight of it nearly cut of Emily's air supply.

They'd moved a table out of the garden onto the beach and the early evening roar of the ocean was their only soundtrack. Emily didn't really know where to begin or what to ask, so she resorted to pushing around a piece of meat on her plate.

"You don't like it?" Marianne's eyes flickered in the light of the oil lamp that dangled from a makeshift stand next to their table.

"On the contrary, really, it's just—"

"Are you nervous?" The kindness oozing from Marianne's face melted Emily's heart. She could feel it turn to liquid in her chest. Where before a hardness had surrounded it, a line of defence she didn't even knew she had, now it all lay open, ready for whatever was to come.

"A little." For the first time, Emily felt her age. Opposite her sat a woman with so many more years of experience in life and love than her, and she thought it best to let Marianne do the talking. Wasn't that what they were here for, anyway?

Not seeming very hungry herself, Marianne shoved her plate away and instead focused her attention on the bottle of beer that accompanied the dish.

"This is all rather romantic, of course." She cast her eyes to the sky above. "It's a full moon as well."

"Perfect," Emily said before nervously taking a swig from her beer.

"I don't know what's going on between us, Emily. I have no idea where you came from all of a sudden and why you make me feel things I haven't felt in a long

time… Well, have *allowed* myself to feel to be more exact."
She gave a tense chuckle. "That kiss this afternoon took
me by surprise and at the same time, it felt as if it was a
long time coming, even though you've barely just arrived."
Marianne bit her lip before continuing. "It takes someone
very special to make me feel like that. I need you to know
that."

Emily nodded. To her surprise, Marianne pushed her
chair back.

"Do you want to go for a walk?"

"I'd love to."

They carried the dishes inside and Marianne locked
the back door before they set off into the darkness.

"I was twenty-five when I met the love of my life."
Marianne's fingers found Emily's in the dark and
entwined themselves with hers. "Her name was Ingrid and
she swept me off my feet. Quite literally. We ran into each
other while both turning a corner in a hurry. At first, I
wanted to yell at this stranger who had the audacity to
steal my precious time—I was that kind of person back
then. But she changed me. Changed everything about
me."

Marianne's fingers gripped tighter. They walked
barefoot along the shoreline, the waves casually licking
their toes.

"I was a junior investment banker and I thought I
was terribly important managing other people's money."
Marianne's tight laugh sounded bitter in the night. "But all
it took to disarm me was a smile." She paused. "Gosh,
that sounds terribly cheesy, but that's how I've always
remembered it."

Marianne pointed at and old overturned boat away
from the shoreline. "Let's sit there for a moment." She
didn't let go of Emily's hand when they approached the
boat and leaned against it for support.

"We fell in love. Made a life together. Were
ridiculously happy together until…" Emily felt her

stomach tighten. Marianne's hand slipped out of her grasp.

"I killed her."

Silence surrounded them. The night was black around them, except for a few night lights of beach houses. Emily thought she had misheard, but then Marianne repeated, "I killed the woman I loved more than anything in this world."

MARIANNE

Marianne felt Emily stiffen next to her.

"It was a car wreck. We were in a crash and it was my fault. I shouldn't have been driving in the state I was in, but I had insisted and we were fighting and I didn't see..." She had to catch her breath. "I didn't see the lorry because I was looking at her, I was berating her for losing money, and when we crashed I hardly had a scratch on me because her side of the car had taken the impact."

Marianne closed her eyes and the tears sprang free. Her voice didn't change pitch and her hands didn't shake, but on the inside, on the back of her eyelids, it was all happening again.

"She died on the way to the hospital." She swallowed away some tears. "And it was my fault. I'd been so angry with her for investing her money in her friend's company after I'd categorically advised her against it— that was my business after all. But that was what she was like. She'd give away her last scrap of clothing to a homeless person. And I was yelling at her about it seconds before she died. It killed her."

Marianne wiped the tears from her eyes, but they kept on coming. "And you know what the police did? They took away my license for a year." She puffed out some air. "That's it. That's how they punish you for killing someone in the motherland."

Emily was eerily quiet beside her.

"God, I'm sorry. I shouldn't have laid this on you. It's not fair and it's not your burden to bear." Marianne wanted to get up and walk away, but she was afraid her legs wouldn't carry her.

"This happened five years ago?" One of Emily's fingers approached her, but Marianne pulled back. She had to. Saying it out loud—after all this time—had convinced her once again that she wasn't worthy to be touched. Especially not by a girl like Emily.

"Yes," came her curt reply.

"And all this time you haven't allowed yourself to be happy for one moment?"

"Of course not." She sniffed loudly, losing all sense of decorum. "Ingrid's dead."

"But it was an accident." Emily's voice sounded thin and insecure.

"An accident I caused."

"But still an accident," Emily whispered, while her hand made another approach. Marianne felt the heat shoot through her and briefly allowed it to warm her up inside.

"I sold everything and moved here." Suddenly, she felt like she needed Emily's touch and she grasped her fingers. "We'd come here on our first big holiday together and we were so happy here. It was the first time I really felt it, that I wanted to spend the rest of my life with her. So, that's what I did. I came back here to mourn her and to make sure I never forget her—nor what I did."

"Jesus."

"Yeah."

They sat in silence for a while. Marianne didn't expect Emily to say anything because what could she possibly say.

"It must seem as if I'm wallowing in self-pity here on my island, some sort of fake exile in paradise, but I needed to do this. I needed to come here. If that makes sense at all."

"I won't claim to understand the extent of your pain, and what happened was terrible." Emily scooted closer and Marianne admired her confidence. "But don't you think you've suffered enough?"

What was enough? Could it ever be enough?

"I don't know. This is my life now. It has its moments, its ups and downs, but not too many. And that's the only way I can live."

Emily brought Marianne's hand to her lips and pressed a tender kiss on it, causing Marianne to retract it instantly.

"It's not the only way. It can't possibly be." Emily was persistent. But what did she know? She was twenty-four years old. Younger even than when Marianne had met the woman she'd spent more than ten years with. She'd just left her fiancé and perhaps that had taken some courage but really, what other choice did she have?

"I hope you understand the reason why I can't—I mean, why this can't go any further. In fact, it has already gone too far." Marianne pushed herself up from the boat. She had enough decency to not leave Emily by herself in the dark. "I'll walk you back."

"Wait." Emily's feet made splashing sounds onto the wet sand.

Marianne turned around to face her. She could barely make out Emily's features in the darkness of the night. It was easier that way. "You don't want to be with me." She tried to stress her point.

"Says who?" Emily's reply came quickly, her voice much harsher than Marianne had expected. "You?" She took a step closer. Marianne could feel her breath float over her cheeks. "And how would you know?" She paused for effect. "And what if I do? What if I really, really want to?"

Marianne had to take a second to let all the questions register. "It's not only up to you."

"Oh, I know that." Was that the blooming barrister coming out in young Emily? "But when you kissed me this afternoon, you didn't leave a doubt in my mind."

"It was a moment of weakness. I—"

"Don't you get tired of this, Marianne? All this defence? All this endlessly feeling sorry for yourself? This blatant refusal to live? You're forty years old, for god's sake. Your life's not over yet."

Marianne started to get annoyed. She hadn't come here to get a talking-to, let alone by someone who'd barely lived at all. "And spending three months on your own in a different continent makes you an expert, does it?"

"No." Emily shook her head. "But it's an easy excuse to hold against me. So is my age. But I saw what I saw in your eyes, Marianne. I saw the desire to live, to feel again. Just… give yourself a chance."

"But that's just it. Ingrid didn't get a second chance, and nor should I."

EMILY

Emily was completely out of her depth, but she felt as though she needed to push. She was fairly certain Marianne didn't take a lot of people on a walk to talk about Ingrid and she needed to make the most of the moment. But years of loneliness and being convinced of her own guilt had obviously made Marianne very stubborn.

"Why did you bring me here?"

"What?" Despite the darkness and the remnants of tears on Marianne's face, despite her reluctance and the fact she obviously clung to any refusal to move on, Emily could still see it in Marianne's eyes. The fire that had blazed in them before she'd leaned in to kiss her. The desire to break free.

"When was the last time you told someone about this?"

"I haven't told…" Marianne hesitated. Emily heard her breathing get back to a more normal rhythm. "A long time."

"Then why did you tell me?"

"Because I clearly owed you an explanation after last night and this afternoon."

"No, you didn't. Not really." Emily wanted to step even closer, wanted to wrap her arms around Marianne and hold her for a long time. "You don't owe me anything. I'm just a guest in the Lodge where you've decided to hide from life."

"You're not just a guest… and you know it."

Relief rushed through Emily. It was true that she was young and her bravest act up until now had been to run away. She'd fled the scene of her crime as well. While she could hardly compare her own anguish to the unbearable pain Marianne must have been in since Ingrid's death, she had a lot of sympathy for the way in which Marianne had decided to cope. But if there was one thing she'd come to accept on this journey, it was that everyone deserves to be happy in their own way and on their own terms.

She inched closer, the heat blazing off Marianne's frustrated body instantly palpable. "Come here, please." She opened her arms and waited for Marianne to accept the invitation. "Please."

There were only two ways Marianne could go. Forward or backwards. If she turned around and went back to the lodge, Emily knew it would be over. If she met her halfway, if she let Emily embrace her, there was a chance.

It took another few long seconds before Marianne finally moved. Tears ran down her cheeks again and her fists were clenched into tight balls. But she made the leap.

She walked into Emily's open arms and allowed herself to be hugged.

Emily curled her arms around Marianne's waist and pulled her close. "Who says you don't deserve to live?" she whispered in Marianne's ear. "Who says you don't deserve it?"

Marianne's response came in long, deep sobs. She relaxed her shoulders and Emily felt her fingers dig deep into the flesh of her back while she cried, raining tears all over her body.

Emily let Marianne cry for a few minutes before gently coaxing her in the direction of the Lodge. She pried the keys from Marianne's jeans shorts, opened the back door—relieved not to find the other guests back yet—and helped a limp Marianne up the stairs to her room.

The scene was a far cry from how she had expected the night to go. Then again, she hadn't really known what to expect, although tales of guilt and death had not exactly been on her mind. A love gone wrong maybe. Or some femme fatale who had broken her heart. But certainly not this.

She looked at the broken woman sitting on the bed in front of her and kneeled down. A tenderness she didn't know she had in her swooped over Emily. She'd only just met Marianne, but she most definitely cared for her in ways she was only just discovering.

What a pair, she thought, as she shifted the sheets to the side and lowered Marianne onto the mattress.

"Stay," Marianne whispered. "Please, stay with me tonight."

Emily shot her a smile, one that even warmed her own heart. "Of course."

She slipped out of her shorts, but kept the rest on, walked to the other side of the bed and climbed in with Marianne. After switching off the lights she slung her arms over Marianne and held her through the night.

Emily barely slept, and she didn't know if Marianne drifted off or not, but they didn't speak. They just lay there, quietly, finding strength in one another's silent company.

Emily knew it was more important than anything else.

MARIANNE

Marianne woke up with her arms around another woman. She blinked against the lingering darkness and made out Emily's blonde mane of hair. She checked the alarm clock on the nightstand and waited for the first light of dawn to filter through the window. The curtains had been left open and soon the room would be bathed in bright light.

Because, this morning, she felt as if she had no real reason not to, she held onto Emily a little while longer. Her head hurt from crying, her nose bunched up and her eyes swollen. Before ticking off her mental to do list—another guest was arriving today, resulting in a full house—she allowed herself a moment to process last night.

She didn't even have to ask herself if something had really—fundamentally—changed. There was another woman in her bed. And although nothing physical had transpired between them, everything was different now because, somehow, Emily had gotten through to her on a deeply emotional level—one she'd considered a no-go zone years ago.

A tween. *Generation Y.* Wasn't that what they were called these days? It just goes to show, she thought, how people can utterly amaze you. She crawled a bit nearer to Emily and pressed her stuffed nose into the girl's hair. Once again, emotion engulfed her, like a shot of heroine in her veins, it seemed to immobilise and entrance her at the same time, until she felt Emily stir beneath her.

"Morning," she whispered.

"What time is it?" Emily's voice sounded as if it needed to be ironed.

"Six." Marianne huddled closer.

"How utterly dreadful." Emily backed up against her, sighed, and went back to sleep. Not a morning person then.

Marianne figured she could forego her morning beach run just this once. What better occasion than a woman in her bed? Now that the room was filled with morning light, her eyes caught hold of the picture of Ingrid and her. And, for an instant, it did feel like a lifetime ago. Marianne was not the same person anymore. She'd changed for the first time after meeting Ingrid. For a second time after the fatal crash. God, how she longed for the next transformation.

Emily's words had kept playing in her mind throughout a fitful night. *Who says you can't be happy?* There was only one person standing in her way, Marianne knew, and it was herself.

In her sleep, Emily turned on her back, her wrinkled face aimed directly at Marianne, forcing a smile to her lips. Then another thought slowly made its way into Marianne's mind.

It was Saturday, August the thirty-first. It was her forty-first birthday. She didn't want a cake, but she knew what she did want.

As if Emily had read her mind while she was sleeping, her eyes flew open. "What day is it today?" she croaked.

"Saturday."

A wide grin appeared on Emily's face. "Looks like you're over the hill then." She pushed herself up, shoving Marianne's arm off her in the process, and straddled her. "Happy birthday." Her eyes sparkled in the golden light of sunrise. She leaned down, her arms resting on either side of Marianne's head, and pecked her softly on each cheek.

Something loosened in the pit of Marianne's stomach, but she had no time to dwell on it.

"What do you want for your birthday?" Emily's tone was not insistent, more probing and careful not to make assumptions.

"You," Marianne replied without hesitation.

"I'll see what I can do." Emily shot her a wide smile. One that dislodged another tight knot deep beneath Marianne's ribcage. She bent her elbows and this time, her mouth didn't aim for Marianne's cheeks. Her lips landed on Marianne's and the kiss sent a spark of desire right up her spine. She responded by grabbing hold of Emily's neck and pulling her close, until she realised that, despite it being her birthday, it was a day like any other at the Lodge.

"I can't... not right now..." She tried to say in between passionate lip locks. "I have guests and—"

"Dao will take care of them. It's your birthday." Emily had stretched her body on top of Marianne's and her nipples pressed into Marianne's flesh. She could hardly argue with that. She tried anyway.

"I have to help her. I'm always there."

Emily nipped at her neck. "Today you're not. And you know what? The place is not going to crumble to the ground. The world will still turn. The guests will not leave."

"God, you're bossy." Marianne couldn't suppress a smile.

"I know." Emily stared down at her with her big blue eyes. "It's one of my quirks."

"Thank you for last night." The words just came. Marianne didn't have to think about them or weigh them. "You've no idea what it meant to me."

"I do." Emily nodded and chewed the inside of her lip.

"You're beautiful and kind and so very thoughtful." Marianne cupped Emily's chin with her hands.

"Oh yeah?" Emily's eyes sparkled. "And you're bloody hot." She bent down and found Marianne's ear. "And I want you so much."

EMILY

Maybe Emily gave the impression that she knew what she was doing, but she didn't have a clue. Her entire body was buzzing, her heart drumming with desire and her blood pulsing with lust. And she really needed Marianne to take charge, but didn't know if she was in the right state of mind to do so.

She'd had the fantasy often, and even indulged in it while lying next to Marianne in her bed last night. A sensual initiation by someone who knew exactly what they were doing. She was twenty-four, formerly engaged and hardly a virgin, but when it came to this, when it came to sleeping with another woman, she might as well have been.

"God, I want you too," Marianne whispered back and Emily felt her body grow rigid underneath hers for an instant. It was only Marianne tensing her muscles so she could topple Emily off of her and take place on top of her.

"You've come here and you've turned my world upside down." Marianne looked down at her, her face still blotched from last night's tears, her hair a mess from sleeping, and Emily felt exactly the same way.

If this was going to be her first time with a woman—and it was—then what could be better than this? It was unexpected, yes, but was she supposed to have planned for it then? And all those thoughts, as meaningful and deep as they were, they dissolved instantly when

Marianne traced a line with her fingertip over Emily's nipple.

"I'll try to go slow." Marianne's voice had grown husky while her fingers drew circles around Emily's nipple. "But it won't be easy." With that, she pinched Emily's nipple between her thumb and index finger, causing Emily's breath to stop in her lungs.

Do whatever you want to me, Emily wanted to say, but the words stayed lodged behind the lump in her throat. With eager fingers, she pulled at Marianne's sleep-crumpled blouse. She wanted it off of her. She wanted skin on skin and fingers on her naked breasts and, more than anything, inside of her.

The blouse was tight and Marianne helped her hoist it over her head. Emily had seen her in a bikini, but it was hardly the same as the white lace bra she was wearing now and she couldn't help but wonder if Marianne had dressed to impress—and if wearing an actual bra for once was part of that plan. Emily fumbled with the lock and held her breath until Marianne's breasts sprang free. Emily had seen naked breasts before, but never like this.

Her eyes locked with Marianne's. She noticed what Emily seeing her naked from the waist up did to her. Emily saw the years of pent-up everything—lust, life, love—flash in the dark of Marianne's eyes. It erupted in the blush on her cheek bones, in the sudden drops of sweat on her forehead, and the raggedness of her breath.

"Take me," Emily said. "Don't go slow on my account. Please."

It seemed as if Marianne had lost the power of speech altogether. As if the time had come for her body to work through it now, to chase away the demons of the past. She tore at Emily's t-shirt and bra, yanking them over her head, causing the entire expanse of Emily's skin to break out in goosebumps.

Marianne's lips captured her left nipple, gently licking it first, before sucking it into her mouth and taking it between her teeth. Emily buried her hands in Marianne's hair, digging her nails deep into her scalp, spurring her on.

Maybe Emily had always known—because how could she not?—but if she didn't, she knew now. Because this was, no doubt, what it was always supposed to have felt like. Fire and abandon. Heat and passion. Desire and emotion crashing together the way their skin did. The way everything about them did.

Emily couldn't stop herself, as if a madwoman had taken possession of her body and wormed her way under her skin. She pushed Marianne's head down, because if no one was going to attend to the mess down there soon, she'd lose all control—and she was already well on her way.

Slow. What a joke.

Marianne caught the hint and kissed her way down Emily's belly. Not with soft pecks, but licking and kissing and biting frantically, because this was as much a first for her as it was for Emily.

She hitched her fingers under the waistband of Emily's panties and tore them off her. Emily greedily helped her by wildly kicking the panties off her legs.

And then there she lay. Naked and wet. Her legs spread for another woman. Her cunt pulsing with need. Watching Marianne as she rested her gaze between her legs made Emily dizzy with desire. Why had she wasted so much time on boys? If a simple look from another woman could make her feel this way?

No time to dwell, because Marianne lowered her head and Emily didn't want to miss a second of that. She flicked her tongue along Emily's pubic hair, planting gentle kisses, inhaling deeply. Emily wanted to scream and beg and plead, but she also knew she had to give this moment to Marianne to truly share it.

The first touch of Marianne's tongue on her clit nearly sent her reeling.

"Oh god," she moaned, her hand searching for something to hold on to. She found Marianne's hand, splayed out on the bed next to Emily's shivering body. She intertwined her fingers with Marianne's while an onslaught of licks and flicks was launched on her clit and pussy lips. Emily didn't know how long she was supposed to last, how long this was supposed to go on for, but her body was already giving way.

She glanced at Marianne's bobbing head between her legs, at their interlocked fingers, at the yellow morning light slanting into the room and she knew this was what she'd been waiting for all her life. This moment. This revelation. This life-changing orgasm.

She came. Hard and quick. Her body spasming while her muscles momentarily lost control. Marianne's impossibly soft tongue on her most intimate parts. And then it was her turn to burst into tears.

She cried for Marianne and for herself. For all she had left behind and for everything that was to come. For the intensity of the moment and the fleeting notion in her mind that everything was possible. If something could feel this good and transformative, anything was possible.

MARIANNE

"Hey." Marianne hurried from between Emily's legs, a bit groggy from the force with which she had clasped them around her head when she had reached her climax. "Come here." She lifted up Emily's head and cradled it in her arms, stroking her hair.

She had probably piled too much on her, possibly taken too much too soon. "Are you all right?" She pressed a kiss onto Emily's hair and waited for her to respond.

"I'm usually not so sentimental." Emily's cheeks moved against her chest when she spoke. "It's just, well, this has been a long time coming for me." She searched for Marianne's eyes as she continued. "No pun intended." The bright smile that shone from her face caused a surge of relief to travel through Marianne's muscles, slackening her posture.

They both broke into a silly chuckle.

"Thank you." Emily freed herself from Marianne's hug. "I guess I really needed that." She straddled Marianne again, just like she had done before. "Just like I need this now." Her golden hair cascaded onto her shoulders and, backlit like that from the ever brighter light streaming through the window, she looked like an angel sent to revive Marianne from the nearly-dead.

Marianne knew what was coming next, and as much as she needed it, both on a physical and an emotional level, a fear still resided in her mind and held her back. Emily kissed her and the fear nearly subsided there and then, but it wasn't enough. Touching someone the way she had just touched Emily was surely an incredibly intimate gesture, but not as intimate as opening yourself up, as spreading your legs the way Emily had done. Marianne wasn't sure she could do it yet, despite the incessant throbbing of her clit and the butterflies fluttering in her stomach.

She pulled back from the kiss, pushing the back of her head into the pillows, and regarded Emily. She looked different, reborn almost, as if, after months of travelling— possibly longer—she'd finally found a home. The fire in Emily's eyes was enough to wash away the insecurities that had crippled Marianne from the inside for so long. Because there were two people in this bed, two people coming home and finding a new lease on life.

Only when it hit her that she was no longer alone could Marianne fully surrender. She let Emily kiss her neck and wrap her lips around her nipples while she stepped out of the mental shackles she had carried around for too long—almost too easily, it felt for an instant—and she let go. She let go when Emily removed her soaked panties and her tongue trailed a moist path along her belly button and then down, and even more so. Marianne let her legs fall wide eagerly by the time Emily's lips reached her pussy and licked her as if she'd never done anything else in her life.

And then, as if nothing was suddenly enough, she gently coaxed Emily's head up and pleaded, "I need you inside of me."

Emily grinned up at her, her chin wet with Marianne's juices—five year's worth of them. She all but licked her lips. And oh, that feeling of being wanted again, of having someone's eyes glint at the prospect of slipping their fingers inside of you, it was almost enough but not quite, because what held Marianne together in that moment, more than anything else, was that she had allowed herself to be wanted again.

Not for long though, because Emily changed position, and Marianne could already feel the tip of a finger circling her entrance. Marianne knew that, once inside, that finger would change everything. It would change her from profoundly untouched and detached, to someone who could love again. Emily's finger slid easily along her wet folds and the connection it established blew Marianne away. It was just a finger, but it healed her and it transformed her in that moment.

"Come here," she called for Emily because she didn't want to be alone in the moment. She pulled her up while her finger remained inside. "More," she said when Emily's face was level with hers.

She slipped in another finger and thrust harder and Marianne had to dig her nails deep into the flesh of Emily's shoulders to hold on, to not be floored by the sheer force of the tiny movements inside of her.

"Oh," she moaned as the flicks of Emily's fingers inside of her seemed to magnify and spread pleasure throughout her body. "Oh yes."

Emily's eyes were on her when she came with a loud gasp. Marianne witnessed how they grew wide as the walls of her pussy clamped around Emily's fingers.

They were silent while Emily gently removed her fingers and Marianne let her body collapse onto the bed—freed and satisfied.

"That was..." Emily still looked down at her, seemingly unable to tear her gaze away. "I don't know. Probably the most amazing thing ever."

"The eloquence of today's youth continues to baffle me." Marianne pulled Emily close for a kiss. She smelled herself when she let her tongue slide between Emily's lips.

"Objection," Emily murmured into her mouth. "Sometimes it's perfectly all right to be stumped for words."

"I could stay here all day," Marianne said.

"Then do." Emily nuzzled her neck. "It's your birthday and it's your house. You can do whatever you want."

And for the first time in years, Marianne felt as if she could.

EMILY

"Do you have any idea how sexy you are with your tight t-shirts and aloof air?" They sat in the shade by the pool. Marianne had called in both of her helpers and instructed them to take care of business today.

"Excuse me?" Marianne's smile had certainly grown wider—as opposed to her t-shirts—and her mannerisms more inviting. Emily had believed her to be quite attractive from the moment they'd met, but now, when she sat with one leg slung over the other, her upper body jammed into a faded black Blondie t-shirt—no bra—and her hair wet from the shower, she looked stunning.

"I don't think you realise how hot you are, so I thought I should tell you." Emily shot her a grin.

"How terribly nice of you." Marianne lifted her sunglasses onto the top of her head. The traces of last night's tears had disappeared and her skin glowed with renewed vigour.

"I just wouldn't want you to feel old and unattractive because you're officially over forty now." She knew she was rambling, making silly conversation to avoid being alone with her thoughts. She felt she had inadvertently stumbled onto someone important here at The Red Lodge, and although her flight back to Bangkok and then to Heathrow wasn't until next Monday—two more nights with Marianne—a sense of dread had already taken root.

She could hardly start talking about the future with Marianne after two orgasms together, nor could she claim to have fallen head-over-heels in love—not out loud anyway—so she had resorted to teasing her.

"No need to worry about that." Marianne kicked the side of her foot against Emily's ankle under the table. "But thanks, anyway."

"Do you know what else we should do for your birthday?" Emily felt like a hyperactive child, but she couldn't stop herself. She scanned Marianne's face for any signs of annoyance, but was only met with tenderness and those smouldering brown eyes.

"What?"

"Get positively plastered." Emily couldn't think of any other way to chase away the malaise in her gut. Well, she could, because what she really wanted to do was take Marianne back to bed, but maybe this morning had just been a one-off for her. Emily didn't really believe that herself, but she couldn't be certain. Also, with last night's confession still fresh on her mind, she felt she needed to let Marianne take the lead.

Marianne regarded her intently. "Okay," she said after a while. "But not here."

Emily had not expected Marianne to agree with her proposal so quickly.

"Let me arrange something. I know the perfect place." She shot up out of her chair, squeezed Emily's knee—a gesture that melted her core like an ice-cube left in the sun—and headed inside.

An hour later they sat on a towel on a tiny deserted beach, dropped off by Dao's husband who was a taxi driver with the promise to pick them up after sunset, and a cooler full of beer by their side.

In London, Emily always drank wine, but in Asia it was often expensive and nothing tasted better than a cool beer after an afternoon in the scorching hot sun.

"If we're lucky, it'll be just us all day." Marianne grinned at her. "A bikini top is not required and skinny dipping is allowed."

"Let's drink to that." Emily took a swig from her beer. It tasted even better today.

"Let me set up this umbrella first and rub some sunscreen on your skin. Three months here doesn't make it less British."

Emily took off her tank and bikini top, lay down on her belly, and waited for the cool lotion to be applied to her sensitive skin.

"You're a proper little madam, aren't you?" Marianne joked as she straddled her behind. "How many nannies and servants did you grow up with?"

Emily didn't want to think about her childhood, nor home. She just wanted to focus on Marianne's hands on her skin. Just being near her aroused her to the point that her bikini bottoms felt drenched all the time.

Marianne made light work of protecting Emily's back from the sun, leaving Emily a little disappointed, until she instructed her to turn around. Marianne lifted her bodyweight off Emily so she could flip her body and lie on her back.

When Marianne sat back down and squirted sun lotion in the palms of her hands, Emily's nipples perked up at the mere sound of it.

"All these foreigners think they can come here and enjoy the beach all day without protection." Marianne started with Emily's shoulders, her touch to-the-point but gentle enough to be a big turn-on. "Then they go back to their hotel in the evening and find their skin full of blisters." Her hands trailed along the sides of Emily's breasts. "Not a pretty sight, I tell you."

What was a pretty sight was watching Marianne from below, her arms strong as she moved her hands along Emily's torso. They ran upwards from her belly to her nipples and stayed there, pinching hard.

"I owe you a slow fuck, I believe." Marianne squeezed her nipples again. "Have you ever done it on a pristine Thai beach, Emily?" A small smile played around Marianne's lips. "It's glorious." She seemed possessed by a new spirit. Someone free and confident and ready to conquer the world. Emily didn't care so much about that world conquering though, as it was mainly herself, her aching, wanting body, that wanted to be conquered over and over again.

She shook her head. She hadn't come to Asia looking for physical enlightenment, but she had a feeling she was about to encounter it.

MARIANNE

Marianne leaned sideways and grabbed an ice cold bottle of water from the cooler. She spilled some on her hands to wash them off as well as the primitive method allowed, then glanced over at Emily's shimmering chest.

Suppressing a grin, she turned her attention back to Emily and slowly, let a few drops of cold water crash down on her nipple. It only intensified the blazing fire in her gaze. She seemed to be down for everything, the recklessness of youth still so present in her soul. Marianne could vaguely remember what it had been like for her back in the day, the excitement of the first time, the anticipation of meeting her first lover—the memory was there somewhere, but just like everything else that would have allowed for careless reminiscing which, in turn, could have caused a ripple of joy to run through her body, she'd buried it somewhere in the back of her mind.

She repeated the process on Emily's other nipple. Emily squirmed a little, her mouth half-open and her breath already being expelled in chopped gusts. Marianne shot her a sly smile, squinting against the reflecting sun on the water behind Emily. She scrambled backwards a bit and let a few freezing drops of water crash down on the panel of Emily's bikini bottoms.

"You're so wet," she said and disposed of the bottle.

Emily looked at her defiantly, as if to say it was all Marianne's fault and she'd better do something about it. Marianne had every intention of doing so. She hoisted her t-shirt over her head and flung it away, not caring where it landed, and stripped off her bikini top before tumbling down onto Emily, their nipples joining in a layer of sunscreen.

Their kiss was instantly deep and passionate, as if there was no more room for mucking about. This was serious, and it showed in the way their lips met.

But how serious could it really be? This was all very idyllic, this fooling around on a deserted beach, but, at its heart—despite the consequences it had on Marianne's wounded psyche—it was nothing but a holiday romance. It had no potential of becoming anything because in a few days Emily would be leaving. And then what? Back to being a recluse? Now that she'd had a glimpse of the real world—the one with real feelings and connections—Marianne wasn't sure she could go back. Still, Emily would be gone. She pushed the thought away. She'd had a lot of practice in doing that.

"Turn around and face the ocean," Marianne whispered. "I want you to see it when I fuck you."

Emily's breath seemed to stop for a split second when she heard Marianne say the word 'fuck'. Marianne didn't figure it was her pronunciation of the word 'ocean' that had that effect. She rolled off Emily so she could swivel around and face the impossible blue of the Pacific just after midday.

"It's gorgeous," she said, an almost pained expression on her face. "But I only have eyes for you." Her hands reached for the back of Marianne's neck and she pulled her on top of her.

Sand grated between their bodies, mixing with sweat and sunscreen, but it all didn't matter. Marianne knew exactly how she wanted Emily. She pushed herself up and started yanking her bikini off.

"Take them off," she instructed Emily. "And come here."

She watched Emily struggle out of her knickers, her coordination obviously hindered by lust and anticipation. Marianne felt it too, that surge in her blood, that uplifting of her spirit, the wetness between her legs, and what could be more beautiful on this planet, she wondered?

She kneeled on the towel and waited for Emily to crawl closer.

"You," she said, when Emily had reached her destination, on her knees opposite Marianne, "are so good for me."

"Jesus," Emily hissed, as if Marianne had just spoken the most erotic words in history, knocking the wind out of her. The following kiss was not a gentle one, it was ravenous, and teeth sank into lips, tongues slipped deep and that's how Marianne knew that this, this very thing happening in front of her eyes—happening to her— would not be something she could walk away from easily.

"I'm going to fuck you," she whispered in Emily's ear, "and I want you to do the exact same thing to me.

Emily nodded, not a hint of insecurity displayed on her face.

Marianne dug her nails into the flesh of Emily's behind, feeling her close, needing her.

It wasn't as if she'd expected anything else, but when one hand traveled to Emily's front, she was astounded by the copious wetness she found between her legs. Marianne had to restrain herself from not plunging in immediately, but she waited for Emily to mirror her movement with her opposite hand. She wanted them to do this together, stroke for stroke.

Marianne let her finger run along Emily's slithering pussy lips, then circled them wide around her clit. When Emily did the same to her, it caused her knees to buckle, but she engaged her core and stayed strong. She could fall apart later.

She let one finger slip between Emily's folds, more probing than thrusting, and to feel a woman in that way again, oh god, tears were already stinging in the corner of her eye.

Emily moaned into her ear, her other hand on Marianne's back for support. And Marianne had truly been convinced that she had banned this kind of closeness from her life for a good reason, but she failed to see it now.

Marianne pulled Emily's head back gently because she wanted to see her face during every second of this act of... of what?

She ignored the question by burying her finger deep inside of Emily's pussy. She just made out the expression of pure bliss on Emily's face before her own air supply was briefly cut off when Emily's finger entered her.

They stared into each other's eyes as they found a rhythm, one of them pulling back as the other thrust deep. Marianne found Emily's clit with her thumb every time she retreated and stroked it gently to the pace at which she fucked her.

Emily, an excellent sapphic student, did the same to her and was bringing her to the brink rapidly. Gusts of breath rushed out of her lungs at irregular intervals. The fire started beneath her stomach and spread quickly, incapacitating her weakening muscles, and all the while, her fingers—two now—stroked the inside of Emily's velvety soft pussy.

And then it was too much. With a whimper and a loud sigh—almost a cry—Marianne came on Emily's fingers just as Emily sighed a loud sigh of relief into her ear.

They crashed onto the towel together, smiling but wordlessly, and Marianne pulled Emily close, as close as she possibly could, because how could she not hold on to that?

EMILY

They'd rinsed off in the sea, re-applied sunscreen— in a chaste way, satiated for now—and sat sipping beer in the shade of the umbrella. Emily tried to appear calm on the outside, but on the inside a whirlwind of emotions slowly started bubbling to the surface.

"Are you having a good birthday?" They'd barely spoken, as if the earlier moment of blind passion could only be revered by muteness.

The smile Marianne shot her was crooked, a bit withdrawn maybe. "I think you know that." She had pulled her knees up and curled her arms around them, as if her body needed protecting from something invisible.

"Was that really your definition of a slow fuck?" Sometimes, Emily had no control over what she said and the words just gushed out. She felt a blush rise to her cheeks as she said it.

Marianne chuckled and shook her head. "Somehow, there's no going slow with you."

Emily could relate. The urgency that rushed through her the instant they touched was staggering. "Maybe... in time."

"Yes, time..." Marianne repeated. "The one thing we don't have."

It was a difficult subject. One that Emily did't even know should even be broached. The facts were simple and clear. The rest far from it.

"Do you ever go back to the UK?" She considered it a fair enough question, not too inappropriate.

"Only when I really have to, which is not very often." She sipped from her beer before continuing. "Not more than once a year, just to check in with my family. To let them know I'm all right. People need to see for themselves once in a while, you know, otherwise they don't believe you."

Emily thought about the vast amount of unanswered e-mails from her mother in her inbox. She should e-mail back later today. She didn't feel as resentful anymore.

"When was the last time?" She secretly hoped it had been more than a year.

"January. I usually go when the weather is most miserable. Just to wallow in it a bit. To feel really cold for once." Marianne had been staring out into the horizon when speaking, but she now turned to face Emily. "What will you do when you get back?"

The unavoidable question. Emily had, first and foremost, run away from the fall-out of her failed engagement, but also from her professional future, which had been mapped out since the day she was born. "Become the solicitor I'm supposed to be, I guess."

"You don't sound very convinced."

"It's just such an inextricable part of the life I had to get away from for a bit. Not necessarily a part I hated, but everything is so intertwined. My family and Jasper's family, they live and work and breathe in the same incestuous circles in London." She hesitated before speaking next. "But I guess it's too early for me to retire to a Thai island."

"You're so young, Emily. You literally have your entire life ahead of you. This is only the beginning..." A sadness had taken hold of Marianne's voice.

"You're only forty-one yourself. You have a whole lot of life to live too." Emily didn't take her eyes of Marianne. "Do you really plan to stay here for the rest of your days?"

"I wasn't really looking ahead so much as to the past." Marianne shrugged. "And what would I do? Go back to investing people's money?" She shook her head. "When I was your age I believed money was everything and I became really good at making tons of it, until I realised it didn't mean a thing."

"Maybe, um, you could find another reason to go back?" Emily tried, her voice sounding smaller than she wanted it to.

Marianne managed a small smile. "Maybe I could." She finished her beer, tossed it to the side and delved into the cooler for another. "Would you like one?"

Emily quickly drained hers, feeling as if she needed it, and nodded.

"I sold everything I had in the UK. Got rid of everything and bought the Lodge. Life is so cheap here, I could easily stay until the day I die and still have a nice sum left." She was staring in front of her again, continuing in a musing tone. "What better way of life is there when you really think about it? No stress. No pressure. Sun. The ocean. No questions asked."

Emily wondered if that was a request, but ignored it anyway. "On the surface, maybe. But don't you want something more... meaningful?"

Marianne sighed before fixing her gaze on Emily again. "Not until now." She swallowed hard. "Not until you came along."

Heat crackled underneath Emily's skin. It was what she had wanted to hear. It didn't change anything fundamentally—nor practically—but she was melting again. "I, uh," she stuttered. "I mean, you make me feel like the person I've always wanted to be. I know we've only just met, but, I just, I don't know…"

"You wonder if there could be something more between us than a few romps on the beach?" It sounded almost cruel when Marianne put it like that.

"Oh, I'm utterly convinced it's already much more than that." Emily didn't back down. She felt ready to fight, as if she had no choice, really.

"Look, Emily." Marianne turned her entire body towards her. "I can fully see why it would feel that way. I mean, look at our surroundings, and yes… we've shared things. You opened up and so did I, and that's incredibly valuable to me—probably more so than you'll ever know—but we must be realistic."

"Yeah… and what does your reality look like?" Emily tried to steel herself, tried not to feel Marianne's words cut through her like a knife.

"This." She opened her arms wide to the ocean. "This is my reality, and from where I'm sitting, it doesn't look too bad."

"So, if I understand correctly, when I leave, I will just have gone and you'll forget about me." Emily's stomach started to knot. She took a few long gulps from her bottle, all but draining it in one go.

"No. I won't forget you. Gosh, how could I?" A mist covered Marianne's eyes. "But you can't possibly believe we have a future together."

MARIANNE

Marianne witnessed Emily's expression change from bravely optimistic to defeated in a split second. But was it not her job, as the older, wiser one, to curtail the enthusiasm of youth in this matter?

"I'm glad I could be of service to you then." More anger crossed Emily's face. She looked around but she had nowhere to go, nowhere to run.

"I'm sorry." Maybe Marianne had been too harsh. She had been out of this game for a long time—and for good reason it seemed now. "But what do you suggest? That I fly back to London with you and we live happily ever after?" It sounded so ludicrous.

"No, of course not… it's just painful to be dismissed like this."

"I'm not dismissing you, Emily." Marianne brought a hand to her heart. "I feel it too. I do. I can feel this beat again," she tapped her chest, "because of you and what you've awakened in me." She felt it all too much, which was the biggest problem. Marianne started to miss the wall she'd built around her and that Emily had started to pick apart. "But I can't possibly, realistically, conceive of the notion of us together in," she curled her fingers into quotes, "'real life'. Not because you're leaving in two days and not because this doesn't mean anything to me, but because of where you are in your life." A chuckle seemed the best way to go.

"Hypothetically, say that I were to go back to London. Regardless of what I'd do there or any of that, do you really think that, in the long run, this could work? I'm your first. And, of course, that feels life-altering. But you have so much else going on. You're not even out. You haven't even started your first job yet. As cliché as it may sound, and I'm just saying it because I feel as if it needs to be said, we are in totally different places in our life."

Tears streamed down Emily's cheeks and Marianne wanted nothing more than to take her in her arms and tell her everything would be all right, but it would be a lie.

"I can't help how I feel," Emily whispered.

"Oh, I know." *So very well.*

Despite herself, she inched closer. Because she couldn't bear this sadness and the sheer unhappiness contorting Emily's pretty face. She couldn't stomach being the source of such misery—again.

"Come here." She crawled over to Emily, on her knees like a toddler, and wrapped her arms around her shoulders.

"What if you did, though?" Emily asked. "What if you tried?"

Marianne chose to kiss away the words. She had no choice. She didn't want to be the cause of more disappointment and she didn't want to lie, so she surrendered to the magnificent physicality that being with Emily represented.

Marianne had been forced to accept the impossible years ago. It wasn't so hard for her now.

She let Emily push her down into the sand, let her run her hands over her already sizzling flesh, but she did it with such unexpected tenderness, her fingers barely grazing Marianne's skin—her actions seemingly so much more considerate than Marianne's—that it reduced her to tears in seconds.

"What a mess," she said into Emily's hair. "I'm so sorry."

"Don't be sorry." Emily planted gentle kiss after gentle kiss on her collarbone, then her cheekbone, her eyes moist but fierce. "It wouldn't be so powerful if it wasn't much more than you make it out to be."

Marianne lay there nonplussed for a second. Where did this girl get all this truth? "You don't give up easily, do you?"

"Not if I really…" She kissed Marianne on the lips. "Really…" The palm of her hand brushed against Marianne's nipple. "Really want something." Her hand trailed down. "And I want you more than anything or anyone I've ever wanted in my short life."

The urgency Marianne had displayed earlier when touching Emily stood in complete contrast to the restraint Emily exercised now.

"And it looks like…" Her fingers trailed along the upper edge of Marianne's pubic hair. "I'm going to have to teach you what a slow fuck is really like."

Maybe Marianne had met her match? Maybe the girl that had swooped in on her own with her over-sized backpack really was meant to come into her life? To change it dramatically.

Emily let her fingers merely dangle between Marianne's legs. "Because let's be honest…" She curled her lips into a smile as she looked down at Marianne, who surrendered willingly. "You don't seem to be very good at that."

Emily fixed her gaze on Marianne while her fingers roamed across the expanse of her skin and, despite the heat, left a field of goosebumps in their wake.

"If you don't want this…" She cupped Marianne's left breast in her hand and squeezed gently. "In your future." Her hand moved more swiftly now, traveling quickly from Marianne's chest to the back of her thighs. "Or this." She angled her hand in a way that made her thumb trail an inch from Marianne's pussy lips. "Well, that's up to you, but…" Her fingers drew circles around Marianne's entrance. "I would appreciate it greatly…" One tip inched closer to tease, then withdrew. "If you let me come to my own conclusions." And again. Marianne's entire body was reduced to a shivering mess, at the mercy of Emily's haunting fingertips. "Speaking of which…" She gave a light chuckle. "Coming, I mean." The blue of everything around them was reflected in Emily's eyes.

"Let's see how long that will take." With that, she entered Marianne slowly with one finger, feeling her way in.

"Oh god," Marianne moaned. She was on the verge already, and it wasn't because Emily added another finger—although that helped—but because of what she said, and how she delivered the words with that unflinching gaze that set Marianne's blood on fire.

EMILY

Emily had yet to encounter a more marvellous sensation than sinking a finger into another woman's wet folds. It was so new, yet familiar and, most of all, so incredibly intimate.

As Marianne groaned herself through climax below her, her body twitching to the rhythm Emily dictated with the thrusts of her fingers, a brand new sense of power descended upon her. To be able to cause Marianne this much pleasure, was such a rush, and the intensity of it all made every sexual encounter with Jasper pale in comparison.

This was much more love-making than she and her ex-fiancé had ever accomplished.

She let her fingers slip out of Marianne gently and brought them to her lips, inhaling Marianne's essence. That, too, made up a brand new, vital experience for Emily. She licked Marianne's juices off her fingers while she kept her gaze fixed on the other woman and she could clearly see the shift in Marianne's eyes. She had surrendered. Maybe only in that moment, but Emily was certain she had seen a glimpse of a future together.

"You." Marianne shook her head. "What are you doing to me?"

Making you feel alive, Emily thought, but she didn't want to push it. Instead, she shot Marianne a smile before planting a kiss on her forehead.

Marianne pushed herself up on her elbows. "I need to cool off for a minute in the sea." She scrambled to her feet. "Alone, if you don't mind." She grabbed Emily's hand, squeezed and brought it to her lips to kiss her palm. "Okay?"

Emily understood. She watched Marianne jog towards the water, her shoulders already heaving from the tears she couldn't hold back.

Emily grabbed another beer and waited patiently for Marianne to process her emotions alone, in the water, where her tears could go unnoticed.

Despite the sudden distance between them, Emily was certain of one thing. She'd never felt as deeply about anyone before in her life. And maybe that was foolish, and purely hormonal, and unrealistic, but so what if it was?

They watched the sun set together, beer in hand, a light buzz glowing in Emily's veins. She wanted to bottle the moment and label it happiness, however fleeting it was. They'd both said their piece and made their point, now they had two days left to mull it over.

Emily had no intention of letting her last two days of holiday go to waste. She wanted to explore every inch of Marianne, wanted to find out as much about her as she was willing to share.

But for now, she remained silent. She allowed Marianne to experience the moment alone but together.

She spent the next two nights in Marianne's bed, discovering erogenous zones she never dreamed she had. She didn't push, nor ask for anything untoward. She gave as much as she could, while enjoying her new-found sexuality, in this little spot of paradise, with this woman who had turned her world upside down.

But on Monday morning, two hours before a taxi was scheduled to pick her up and drive her to the airport, she had to ask.

They'd barely slept, the urgency of Emily's approaching departure keeping them awake between fitful bouts of half-sleep and mindless, excessive groping at each other. Wanting it all, but knowing full well it was all about to slip away.

"Tell me honestly." Emily turned on her side and watched Marianne stretch out like a cat. "Will I ever see you again?" Her heart beat nervously in her throat, thrashing about like a petulant child who is denied her favourite piece of candy.

"Yes, of course. I just—I don't know when." Marianne brought a finger below Emily's lip and stroked her there. "I'll plan a visit to London really soon, I promise."

Emily wanted to protest and hug Marianne at the same time. As the last two days had progressed, her desire to fight had been eclipsed by the emptiness that had expanded inside her chest as the moment of her departure came closer. It wasn't as much acceptance as it was sheer dread. The fear of losing something so important so quickly.

"Sooner than January?"

Marianne nodded. "Yes, much sooner."

"And you'll Skype and e-mail and Whatsapp me?" She felt like a needy teenager then.

"Every day."

Somehow, the easy terms with which Marianne agreed seemed more like hollow words than promises.

"I don't want to go. I mean, after three months away from everyone, my friends and my family, I was expecting to be so much more excited to go back, and before I came here, I was, but now I just want to stay here with you."

"Sweet girl," Marianne said. "You've done so much for me."

But what will you do for me? Emily didn't dare say it out loud. On the one hand, it wasn't fair, and on the other, she was afraid of the answer.

"You'll be all right. Once you see your loved ones again, you'll feel right back at home."

"I guess I'd best start packing, make sure I don't forget anything."

"If you do, I'll deliver it personally." Marianne rolled on top of her, pinning Emily's arms above her head. "Now it's time for my goodbye kiss." She wrapped her lips around Emily's right nipple and sucked hard.

MARIANNE

Marianne helped Emily haul her huge backpack into the boot of the taxi and then she watched her leave. She stood on the curb for a long time, gazing at the empty spot the car had left. *Can five days change your life?* Once, a split second had changed her life, so yes, five days could definitely do the trick.

The real task at hand, though, was to figure out her true feelings for Emily. She didn't want to rush into booking a flight to London without assessing the consequences of the mind-blowing sex they'd had. They'd had conversations as well, but mostly sex. Or maybe intimacy was a better word. Either way, Marianne's world had been thoroughly rocked. Her life shaken upside down. And now what?

Was she in love? They'd both danced around the word carefully, making sure to not even come close to pronouncing it—the utter foolishness of it, really.

But was she?

Only time could tell.

She went about her business the way she had done before Emily had turned up. And then time told her. Through a longing so acute it kept her awake at night in her empty bed. She didn't know which picture to stare at most. The one of her and Ingrid on the mantle, or the one

Emily had snapped of the pair of them on the deserted beach before things had gotten too intense.

The past or the future? What did she choose?

She'd chosen the past long enough.

Three weeks after Emily had left, she booked a return flight from Bangkok to London, but she didn't tell Emily just yet. She needed to know what it would be like to arrive in London again, if it would be different this time. If the air around her would be lighter or if everything would still remind her of that one night.

She booked herself into a hotel like she always did, not wanting to impose on estranged—by choice more than anything—friends and family. Being away from the self-created safe haven that her house on Samui represented was challenging enough, and not having any privacy to speak of only made it more so.

In the beginning, when she returned the first few times—more frequently because there were still loose ends to tie up—she had to explain herself over and over again to vexed family members who seemed endlessly offended by the fact that she chose an impersonal hotel room over their hospitality. But they were used to it by now. Everyone can get used to almost anything.

The first thing she did—she always did—after settling in, was to visit Ingrid's grave. It had become a ritual now, more than a need begging to be met, more than penance, but it had to be done. She had to stand in front of it and say the words.

She took a ridiculously expensive cab, paying—quite literally—ten times more than in any Thai city, to the cemetery, pulled up the collar of her coat against the cold wind and made her way onto the grey stone path that led to the spot where the love of her life lay buried.

"I'm sorry," she said, to the marble headstone, "I'm so sorry." As if it could change anything at all. As if the words were not the most over and falsely used ones in the history of humankind. But she said them anyway because there really was nothing else she could say—or do.

She'd run, she'd hidden herself away, she'd taken the blame and torn herself away from anyone else that mattered—anyone who could even remotely make her feel better. It would never be enough, because it would never give Ingrid her life back, but, in the aftermath, after it had happened and Marianne had watched the ambulance drive off while Ingrid was still alive—barely, but still—only to find she had passed when she reached the hospital, it was all she could do.

Marianne waited for the tears that always overtook her at this point. She waited for the year's guilt that had amassed in her soul to find its way out, not to relieve her, but to remind her. But her cheeks stayed dry, and that was how she knew.

In the taxi back to the hotel, she scrolled through the dozens of pictures Emily had sent her since she'd returned home. She'd documented her entire life over the phone. Shots of her in bed just after she woke to show Marianne that she was the first thing on her mind in the morning. Photos of Emily before bed without any clothes on. A picture of Emily and the kitten she'd adopted days after her arrival because she didn't want to be so alone.

"Turning into a crazy lesbian cat lady already?" Marianne had texted.

Emily had responded by sending her a pouting selfie with the caption: "Without you here I just might."

While she took a shower, Marianne pondered her next move. Emily had sent her address in case she wanted to send her something via snail mail. A smile broke on her face when she decided what to do next. A smile that would never have made its way through the gloom on previous visits to London.

EMILY

Emily had taken the position at her father's firm. She loved the law and she wanted a job, the only downside was having to work alongside her family all day. Theoretically, she could have waited for a bout of divine inspiration, a metaphorical voice descending from the heavens to tell her all about her future, but, frankly, if she had to stay home one minute longer than she had to these days, she went crazy.

Nights were the worst. After a mere three nights in Marianne's bed, she had trouble sleeping alone in her London flat.

She'd fielded everyone's questions expertly, as if she were already a practicing solicitor, because what could she say? "Oh hey, I met someone. A forty-one year old recluse living in Thailand. Oh, and she's a woman. We spent five days together and it changed my life."

Where Emily came from, no matter how true and how much she felt it, things like that were never, ever said. And if they were, they'd be dismissed as a folly, a silly dalliance.

"Oh, the tales Emily has to tell about her travels. Madness." Emily could hear her mother's voice in her head.

So, she'd kept Marianne a secret. Maybe it would be different if she were there, but she was miles away. Not a word had been said about a potential visit. Emily was afraid to ask, and she guessed Marianne didn't want to get her hopes up before she actually made a decision.

Emily had been on the job for only two weeks. It wasn't raining, so she decided to walk home instead of cramming herself between a sea of people on the tube. She took on a brisk pace because she was anxious to cuddle Archie, who'd been alone in her flat all day.

She checked her phone for new messages or e-mails the way she always did, but it was well past midnight in

Thailand and Marianne would be fast asleep. She'd barely heard from her in the past two days and an unspoken dread had settled in the pit of Emily's stomach. She'd send Marianne some pictures later so she could wake up with a smile.

Due to the seven-hour time difference with Thailand, evenings were hard for Emily. By the time she got home from work, Marianne was unreachable. Emily tried to get up earlier in the morning to fit in a quick Skype chat, but she was always so groggy, having never been a morning person, that they'd soon decided against making a habit of it.

They were in touch though, and that was something. Emily had feared Marianne would be quick to go back to her hermit, no-contact-with-the-motherland ways, but she sent her pictures and sweet good morning messages. It was hardly enough, with so little to look forward to. Emily had checked out flights to Bangkok for Christmas, but they were hideously expensive and she'd only have a few days off—even less if she told her father the real reason she already wanted to go back.

It was all in Marianne's hands now.

Emily trudged along and enjoyed being outside. It was a twenty-minute walk from the Kane & Associates office to her flat, and she needed the exercise, the feeling of doing at least something physical. Her body had been sorely neglected of late, and cyber sex was such a dud. Emily had only just experienced the hands of a woman on her skin, and now she had to make do with merely imagining them again? How did she find herself in a secret, lesbian, long-distance relationship anyway? And was it even a relationship?

She was getting pretty riled up and picked up the pace. She'd need to look into that gym membership her mother kept talking about. She was practically jogging when she turned the corner to her street. She slowed down when she caught sight of her building and let her body relax, anticipating Archie's high-pitched meows upon her entering the flat. Maybe she *was* turning into a crazy cat lady.

Emily's flat took up the two top floors of a terraced house that belonged to her family. Her cousin Laura occupied the ground and basement floors. Who was that hunched against the facade? Not Seth, Laura's boyfriend who always lost his keys, Emily hoped. She didn't like him—or better put, he didn't like her so much anymore since she'd broken up with his best buddy Jasper a month before their wedding. She could hardly blame him for that, but still, she absolutely didn't feel like having to engage him in small talk if even for a minute or two.

Upon closer inspection, that wasn't a man's figure. Emily blinked once, twice. Was she dreaming? She broke back into a jog, her heart hammering frantically in her chest, and not because of the sudden change in pace she subjected her feet to.

"Hey stranger," Marianne said, half her face covered by the collar of a thick overcoat.

"Oh my god." Emily dropped her purse on the floor, shook off her disbelief, and wrapped her arms around Marianne.

"Surprise," Marianne whispered in her ear.

MARIANNE

The tears that hadn't come when she'd visited Ingrid's grave, now found a way out easily, wetting Emily's hair and coat. She still had the same effect on her, ridding her of years of guilt and shame in an instant.

"I missed you so much." Emily held on tight. They'd never hugged with so many layers of clothing between them, and it was so cold out on the street.

"Aren't you going to invite me in?" Marianne wiped away most of the tears with the back of her hand while she let go of Emily.

"Yes, yes," Emily stuttered while scrambling for her bag, and Marianne thought it was the most adorable sight she'd ever seen.

Marianne took a deep breath while Emily fumbled with the key in the lock. Her plan obviously had not missed its effect.

"I can't believe it," Emily rambled on as they climbed up the stairs. Once there, she had another lock to struggle with. Her hands were trembling so hard, she didn't manage to slip the key in.

"I'll do it." Marianne put her hand on Emily's and took the key from her. She let them in and they were greeted by the cutest ginger kitten. He jumped up and down and tried to climb up their legs.

Marianne crouched down to pet him, but Emily didn't agree.

"Hey." She seemed to have recovered from the shock. "I know he's a furry little casanova, but humans first."

Marianne smiled up at her, lust and happiness and pure joy bursting through her veins. She shot up from kneeling next to the kitten, quickly got rid of her coat, and pushed Emily against the door.

"You were right all along," she told her as she pulled at the buttons of her jacket. "We have to try."

Emily just looked at her with hungry eyes. A look that sent a bolt of lightning straight up Marianne's spine. She needed to feel skin, needed to disappear into this moment of reunion. They could talk later.

"Don't you dare go slow now," Emily whispered, her voice just ragged breaths.

Marianne yanked Emily's overcoat off her, tore at the navy pin-striped blazer she wore underneath, and started undoing the buttons of her starched white blouse.

Her clothes may have been different, her hair styled for a corporate life, but her eyes were the same, and the skin underneath the layers of fabric, although definitely paler than when Marianne had last seen it, once released, felt like home.

Marianne paused before launching herself at Emily's bra. She took her time to take in the sight of a blushing Emily, sandwiched between her and the door. She wore a simple white bra with a bit of lace trimming around the top edge. Her face was make-up free, and rightly so because she didn't need any cosmetics to enhance it.

"You're beautiful," Marianne said as she pulled the double layer of jumpers over her head, exposing a faded black Velvet Underground t-shirt underneath. Emily's hands lunged for it instantly.

Marianne let her tear it off her. She didn't wear a bra.

Emily seemed to have trouble suppressing a smile, but even more than that, her face displayed pure lust.

Marianne pressed her naked chest against Emily and kissed her. She tasted vaguely of coffee and mints, and everything fell away. The doubts, the hesitation, the reasons for not booking a flight immediately.

Marianne trailed her hands from Emily's neck, over her throat, to her bra, where she lifted a soft breast out of its cup. Her fingers found a nipple and squeezed. She wanted to taste it, but couldn't tear her lips away from Emily's just yet.

Emily's hands found their way between their bodies and, in her more gentler way, rolled her fingers over Marianne's nipple.

She felt it so clearly then, rushing through her, that she couldn't hold in the words. Marianne broke their lip lock and regarded Emily. Her lips were parted and her eyes half-lidded, but the blue still shone through.

"I'm so in love with you," she said, and it didn't feel foolish or rushed.

"Oh," Emily groaned, as if Marianne had just pinched her nipple again. She pulled her close, her hands in Marianne's hair, and kissed her with such fervour it didn't leave any room for doubt about how she felt about that.

"Fuck me, please," Emily hissed into Marianne's mouth.

"Really?" Marianne smiled. "That's your response?"

"It's the only one I have right now." Emily zipped down her trousers, pure need blasting from her eyes.

Marianne understood that, in certain moments, it was the only way in which to express love.

She kissed Emily again, their tongues meeting for long seconds, teeth sinking into sucked-in lips, only coming up for air because they had to. Marianne's right hand made its way down to the waistband of Emily's panties, but Emily was impatient, curled her fingers around Marianne's wrist and guided her hand all the way down in one go.

There's wet and there's wetter, Marianne thought, as her fingers met Emily's drenched pussy lips. She didn't tease, just plunged in, two fingers at once.

"Ah." Emily banged the back of her head against the door, which made the kitten at their feet mewl in distress. "Oh god."

Marianne thrust up and down, her movements restricted by Emily's panties, which didn't seem to bother Emily much. She saw no reason to draw it out too long, Emily had waited long enough. She let her thumb flick over Emily's clit and the effect was instantaneous.

Marianne tried to remember if she'd ever seen a need so big, a desire so on display in someone's eyes, etched on the mask of their face, expressed through the trembling of muscles.

She stroked and circled, flicked and thrust, until Emily's body twitched against hers and went still for an instant, after which she collapsed in Marianne's arms.

EMILY

"I love you," Emily said with the last of her strength. The climax had been as strong as it had been quick, ripping through her like an electric current—three weeks worth of sexual tension, amped up by topless phone pictures and raunchy texts, steamrolling through her body. She needed to sit down.

"I've got you." Marianne curved an arm under Emily's armpits and held her up. "God, I've missed you."

Emily drew in a few deep breaths before speaking. "I can't believe you just turned up like that." They still stood huddled together against the door, Archie trying to jump up their legs.

"Would you like me to go?" Emily felt Marianne's lips stretch into a smile against the skin of her neck.

"I want you to stay forever, more like." She pulled her close, determined to never let go of her again.

"Maybe you should feed your cat." Marianne kissed her on the bottom of her chin. "What a feisty little thing… he reminds me of someone."

"How long are you staying?" Emily hoped in vain that Marianne had booked an open-ended ticket, but, despite not having met her that long ago, already knew her well enough.

"Two weeks. I can't close the Lodge for much longer than that."

"Where are you staying?"

"A hotel in Queensway. I always—"

"Please, come stay with me. If you leave in two weeks, I need you here with me until then."

"Don't worry, I'll be here." Marianne pecked her on the cheek. "Shall we sit for a minute?" She stepped away from Emily—and already felt too far away—to pick up her t-shirt. She quickly flung it over her head before picking up Archie.

"But I haven't touched you yet."

Marianne shot her a wide grin. "Unlike you, I can wait."

"We'll see about that in a moment," Emily shot back. She headed into the kitchen to fill Archie's plate with fresh food. After washing her hands, she joined Marianne in the sitting area.

"Posh place for an early twenty-something."

"If you have to come from a moneyed, conservative, stiff upper-lipped family, you may as well enjoy the few perks it has to offer."

"Speaking of which… when will you introduce your older lesbian lover to them?"

"If I'd known you were coming I would have organised afternoon tea, obviously."

Marianne stretched out her arms and pulled Emily toward her. Emily only now realised her chest was only covered by a topsy-turvy bra and her zipper was still open. She landed with the back of her head on Marianne's thigh, looking up into her wondrous yellow-speckled brown eyes, giving Marianne's hands free reign over her exposed torso.

"This is real, right? I'm not hallucinating?"

"Is that an invitation to pinch you?" Marianne smiled down at her, her hand already grazing the swell of her breast.

"As if you need one."

"True." Marianne bent down and kissed Emily on the nose as she slipped a hand under the cup of her bra and found her nipple.

"Aw," Emily mock-complained. Heat surged in her belly again. She couldn't wait any longer. She needed to feel Marianne's flesh tremble at the touch of her finger, needed to taste her between the legs.

She pushed herself off Marianne's leg and flipped over on her knees. "Enough of that already." She painted a wicked grin on her face. "Time to make another pussy meow."

Marianne chuckled and shook her head. "Oh, baby."

The unexpected term of endearment threw Emily off her game somewhat, but the sight of Marianne's nipples poking through the flimsy fabric of her t-shirt was enough to keep her focused on the task at hand. She slipped her palm under Marianne's thigh and pulled so she landed flat on her back on the couch.

"Should I not take my shoes off?" Marianne asked. "Wouldn't want to get your Laura Ashley sofa dirty."

Emily crawled on top of her. "I'll shut you up soon enough." She hoisted Marianne's t-shirt up and exposed her breasts. They were tanned—no lines—and Emily wondered if she'd been back to 'their' beach. She leaned over and took a nipple between her lips, sucking it into her mouth. After flicking her tongue over it, she looked up and found Marianne's eyes. "Let's see just exactly how long you can wait."

Marianne's eyes had lost focus already, it was all hunger and need swimming in the brown of them now.

Emily made her way down, leading with her mouth. She kissed a moist path to Marianne's belly button, letting her tongue explore there. Oh, how good it felt to taste her, to smell her, to touch her. As far as Emily was concerned, this was a dream. A beautiful real one she didn't have to wake up from. She opened the button of Marianne's jeans and pulled them down, no longer able to wait. Three weeks was long enough. After what Marianne had made her feel in Thailand, it was all she'd been thinking about. Marianne was already busy heeling her shoes off, because those pants had to come off completely. Emily needed to see her there. She wouldn't be satisfied with just copping a feel with her finger. She wanted it all now.

It took a minute before they'd gotten all of Marianne's clothes off and she lay naked and spread out in front of Emily. At last, she thought, and started by planting a line of kisses on Marianne's inner thigh.

The smell of her was intoxicating, like nothing Emily had ever smelled before she'd met her.

MARIANNE

Marianne would never forget why she had denied herself an emotional connection with another person for so long, but, as she lay there at Emily's mercy, waiting for the first contact of her tongue with her aching, throbbing clit, she was relieved to have allowed Emily into her life. She could hardly escape the raw, physical aspect of what was going on between them, but it was so much more than that. And she'd said the words now. She wouldn't have said them if she didn't mean them. Emily's lips inched closer to her pussy. Marianne's skin seemed to catch fire in every spot where Emily's mouth left a moist mark. She had to resist the urge to pull her close, to pull her on top and touch her wherever she could, but she had to give Emily this moment, and she gladly did. Marianne knew what it was like to look down upon a lover the way Emily did now. How it felt when someone opened up for you completely, offered herself to you. She put herself, and her pleasure, at Emily's mercy, and she felt privileged to do so.

Emily's tongue grazed her outer lips softly. God, she had such a gentle touch. She didn't rush—and she definitely liked to tease. Whereas Marianne, every time she touched Emily, was overcome with such urgency, such a fear of everything slipping away in an instant again, that hurrying things along in a frenzy of blinding want was her only option.

It was yet another reason why Emily was good for her.

Emily's tongue slithered along her clit now, so light Marianne could barely feel it, but she felt every little thing Emily did as if it was magnified by a force of a million.

"Oh," she moaned, another something she had to get used to again. The sound of her own pleasure. Not easy when you've been mute for years.

Emily flicked again, still teasing, still leaving enough time between licks for Marianne to recover. When Emily sucked her bloodshot bud between her lips without warning though, a tremor moved like an earthquake through her muscles, shattering every resolve, every little piece of resistance Marianne had so carefully built up.

She did it again and Marianne recognised that falling feeling. The sensation of not having a choice but to go with was happening to your body and knowing that, no matter what, you were in safe hands. She hadn't seen the addition of fingers coming. Emily pried at her entrance for an instant, immediately slipping in. She dug deep and sucked hard on Marianne's clit while her tongue flicked and flicked. Marianne fell. She fell through space and darkness, through years of punishment and emotional abstinence.

"Oh baby," she cried, when she came to again, her muscles going limp while Emily thrust one more time with her finger.

Emily slipped her finger out gently and crawled up to her. "We're going to have to work on your stamina because I think you just set a new record."

"It's not me," she said, while exhaling deeply. "It's you."

"How original." Emily let her body crash down on Marianne's, who wrapped her arms around her.

"Excuse me, but I'm not exactly firing on all cylinders at the moment."

"Excuses, excuses..." Emily sank her teeth softly into Marianne's neck. "I'm so happy you're here."

"I'm delighted I came."

"Funny." Emily pushed herself up again and they looked at each other. Emily had an expression of pure bliss on her face, her hair lit up by the light of a street lamp outside, her eyes twinkling with satisfaction.

"You must be hungry." Marianne had only eaten a muffin when she got off the plane, her stomach too jittery for a big lunch. She was also starting to feel the jet lag.

"No." Emily smiled. "I just ate."

After ordering pizza and devouring it quickly, as if eating was a waste of time, Emily took Marianne by the hand and led her to the bedroom. The sight of a real bed, as opposed to an airplane seat, made Marianne's tired muscles tingle with delight.

"If I lie down now, I won't wake up until the morning." She stood behind Emily and hugged her, her hands clasped together over her belly, inhaling the scent of her hair.

"Are you feeling your age?" Emily rubbed her behind against Marianne's hips. "Your loss, old-timer."

"I truly don't remember you having such a mouth on you at my place."

Emily let her head fall back onto Marianne's shoulder. "I'm on home turf now. I have the advantage."

"What else do you have?" Too tired to stay standing, Marianne moved to the edge of the bed, sat down and looked around the room. "Anything interesting hidden in one of those drawers?"

"Maybe…" Emily headed to the other side of the bed and pointed at the bedside table. She sat down and painted a dejected pout on her face. "But I'll show you tomorrow because you're too tired now."

Marianne smiled. "Show me now, please." She rolled onto the bed, wearing just her t-shirt and a pair of shorts Emily had lent her.

"Are you sure? I mean, I wouldn't want you to miss your sleep… Once you see what I have in there, you may want to stay awake for a while."

Marianne crawled on top of her and then over her, extending her arm to reach the drawer Emily was referring to. "Yes," she mumbled, "I'm sure." She was also intrigued. Emily hadn't been expecting her, so she wondered what it could possibly be.

"Open it," Emily said. Marianne lay with her head facing away from Emily, but she picked up on the sudden tremble in her voice. She turned around to look at her and found Emily sporting a healthy blush.

EMILY

Emily's cheeks flushed, which was to be expected, but she hadn't had time to prepare for this moment—though she'd spent many hours awake at night thinking about it. She had no idea this opportunity would have presented itself so quickly, but could only be excited that it had—and that she'd had the nerve to go late night shopping last week.

"Go on," she egged Marianne on. "Open the drawer."

Marianne bit her bottom lip, curiosity glinting in her eyes, before turning around and reaching for the handle of the drawer.

When she opened it, something started tingling in Emily's belly—the same excitement as when she'd purchased the item, and then later, at home, had tried it on for the first time. Idly, because there was no one to use it on.

Emily couldn't see Marianne's face as she caught sight of it, but she saw her body convulse with giggles.

Marianne flipped back over holding a rather sizeable blue dildo and a strap-on harness. Her eyebrows were arched up—in surprise, amazement, disgust? Emily had no idea.

"Emily Kane…" Marianne's voice dripped with lust, all gooey and low. "Well, I never…"

Emily knew that if she wanted to be the one to use the contraption, she couldn't just sit there looking smitten and subdued. She had to take charge. "I want to fuck you with it." She put her hand on Marianne's—the one holding the toy. "Sooner rather than later."

Marianne obviously couldn't wipe the puzzled look of amazement off her face. "How presumptuous." She chewed on her lip again.

"You can sleep on it, if you want." Emily tried to inject a casualness into her voice she was not feeling at all.

"That can't be very comfortable." Marianne drew her lips into that crooked grin. She deposited the dildo and harness on the pillow next to her, and dragged Emily on top of her. "And I don't need to sleep on anything." She kissed Emily's doubts away—not doubts about what she wanted, but about how this would all go down. "I want you to fuck me," she whispered in Emily's ear, her breath hot and moist. "Tonight."

Emily's mind blanked and her body turned to liquid. She realised she'd have to keep it together a bit more if she was to live her fantasy—however much by surprise it had taken her.

Emily disappeared into the bathroom with the toys. She took a shower and slowly towelled off, not rushing, but trying to enjoy the moment. She didn't want to waste too much time either, for fear jet lag would win and Marianne would nod off.

But she needn't have feared. Apparently, the prospect of what was about to happen was enough for Marianne to kick her fatigue to the curb. She looked rather invigorated when Emily stepped back into the room, blue dildo standing proud between her legs.

When she'd tried it on out of curiosity, alone in her room, the first time, she'd already revelled in the immediate sense of power it seemed to instill her with. Now that Marianne was in the room with her, ready to receive, it made her blood sizzle in her veins. This was her first time, but Emily knew exactly what to do, as if the knowledge just came with possessing the toy—with strapping it on.

She approached the bed, where Marianne lay watching her, a curious but enthralled expression on her face—lips slightly parted, eyes slitted together.

"I hope this thing comes with lube," Marianne joked.

"Of course," Emily was quick to say.

She'd been too bashful to ask for a lot of information in the shop, but she'd been prepared enough to buy lube in the process. She knew that much.

"You look so... incredibly hot right now. You should see the look in your eyes, babe."

Emily didn't need to see it. She felt it. That surge to take command—to take Marianne. If only it could make her stay.

"Come here." Marianne offered her hand to Emily, who took it and used it for leverage to climb onto the bed.

"Not too tired then?" Emily teased.

"Clearly, you have resourceful ways of keeping me awake."

Emily tried to do the calculation in her head, but time differences always made her brain freeze. She knew it was late for Marianne's body though, or early, depending on how you looked upon it.

"After this, you can sleep in my arms. I'll be by your side all night." Emily went a little weak at the knees at the thought of waking up next to Marianne in the morning.

Marianne curled her fingers around Emily's neck and pulled her in for a kiss. It was oddly exciting to lie on top of her with the dildo taking space between them.

It didn't take long for their kisses to transform into a frenzy of hungrily sucking lips and grazing teeth. Emily pulled Marianne's Velvet Underground t-shirt over her head again and quickly disposed of the flower-patterned pink shorts she'd lent her. And then Marianne lay naked in front of her, not for the first time today, but this time couldn't be more different.

Emily began by kissing every inch of Marianne's skin. She covered her in soft peck after soft peck, first her neck, then her collarbones and her breasts. She loved taking her time and seeing how Marianne reacted—mostly by squirming beneath her, her body twitching and her moans encouraging. The woman really did need to work on her patience.

Before assuming her position between Marianne's legs, she grabbed the bottle of lube from the night stand and took it with her.

She'd sat in between Marianne's legs before—and it was always a deeply erotic and emotional experience—but this time there was an added bonus in the shape of a dildo.

MARIANNE

When Marianne had disembarked from the plane that morning, she'd never have thought she'd be in this position later that night. She remembered the excitement of using toys, but, and Emily had no way of knowing this because they'd hardly had time to discuss it, she'd only been on the receiving end a few times.

Ingrid loved receiving, demanded it really, and Marianne happily obliged. She knew exactly—well, she could have a good guess at it anyway—how Emily felt right now, and this was an experience she'd never want to rob her of.

She liked this side of Emily, the playful, surprising, knowing-exactly-what-she-wanted side. And she gladly spread her legs for her.

Emily's hands trembled a bit when she squirted some lube into her palms, but Marianne suppressed the urge to help her. This was her show. It was important to leave her in command.

Emily's hands reached Marianne's soaked pussy—hardly in need of lube at all, but it's always better to be safe than sorry—and her long fingers spread the liquid over her lips, mixing it with her natural juices.

Marianne watched how Emily applied the lube to the dildo with suggestive strokes of her hand. Bubbles of desire burst in her blood. She hadn't seen anything more exciting in the last decade of her life, maybe never.

There sat this innocent-looking young woman with curly blonde hair and shimmering blue eyes who'd come into her guesthouse one day and changed everything, rubbing her hands over a glistening silicone cock. A shiver ran up Marianne's spine. She didn't have to wonder if this was what happiness felt like. She knew.

Emily ran her lubed-up hands over the inside of Marianne's thighs, tickling and teasing.

Marianne tried to keep the words from rolling off her tongue, but as had become a habit when she was with Emily, she couldn't stop herself. "Fuck me, baby," she said, and the words roused even more lust in her blood. "Fuck me."

Emily looked at her from under hooded eye-lids, as if to say, "You're not in charge now. I choose what happens and if I choose to wait, you wait." She let the tip of her finger slip inside Marianne, then another.

In any other circumstance, it would have been enough for Marianne, but she knew what was yet to come, and her body started shaking at the mere thought of it.

Emily casually slid two fingers in and out of Marianne's lubed-up pussy, all the while keeping her eyes—with that look—on Marianne. Maybe she was still trying to make a point, but Marianne was getting past anything that required logical thought.

When she let her fingers slip out, leaving Marianne empty and craving so much more, the intensity in her gaze changed. She crept closer on her knees, until Marianne could feel the tip of the dildo touch her lips.

"Oh god," she moaned, already.

Emily circled her fingers around the shaft and guided the tip along Marianne's slit, up and down, briefly teasing her clit before trailing to her entrance. She didn't enter just yet though—that would not have been taunting enough. She repeated the process, this time circling the tip around Marianne's clit twice before heading back down. But then, she acquiesced. Slowly, the head slipped in, opening Marianne up in ways completely forgotten to her. Deeper it went, and then a bit more, and then so deep Marianne seemed to be filled to the brim, no room for anything else, every nerve in her body focused on that spot, on the object inside of her, and the gentle thrusting motion it started to make.

Emily lowered herself gently onto Marianne, her body weight resting on her arms planted next to Marianne's head. She locked her gaze on Marianne, a look in her eyes Marianne had not yet encountered before, and fucked her. Fucked her slowly at first, letting Marianne get used to so much otherness inside of her—although, despite it being a toy, it couldn't have felt more like an extension of Emily's body. She slowly amped up the rhythm, leaving Marianne gasping for air.

She'd surrendered to Emily before, but not like this. While Emily thrust inside of her, opening her up in what was physically her most intimate spot, Marianne's heart started to truly recover—to open up as well. She could see it then, the two of them together.

"Oh," she moaned, and her head shook a little from left to right of its own accord, with disbelief and surprise and complete capitulation.

The tears came before the contractions in her muscles. They streaked Marianne's heated cheeks as her body shook with the force with which she met Emily's strokes.

She wanted to tear her gaze away from Emily's, but she couldn't. The look in Emily's slitted eyes was as much a part of her climax as all the rest that was taking place in that moment. Emily's jaw had dropped, leaving her mouth slightly open. Beads of sweat pearled on her forehead, her body not used to these kinds of movements perhaps. Her breath came with a heavy and slow gust every time she spread Marianne a little wider, letting herself in a little bit more.

"Oh baby," Marianne shrieked, having lost control of her voice. "Oh jesus."

It started at her core, a simmering fire that, in a matter of seconds, transformed into an obliterating blast, reaching the tips of her toes and fingers, making them curl with satisfaction, with every delicious thrust of Emily's pelvis against her own.

Orgasms could differ so much, Marianne knew—able to adequately give herself one in the space of two minutes with a few well-aimed flicks of her fingers—and this one would change everything. Again.

EMILY

Emily had never seen such a mixture of desire and despair in someone's eyes, but she hadn't hesitated when Marianne had started to cry. She hadn't stopped because she knew she had to get her through this—and doing what she was doing now, a foreign object strapped to her thighs, seemed to alter the emotions on Marianne's face by the second.

She bent her elbows a little more, changing the angle of the toy inside Marianne slightly and was met by another guttural groan. Her nipples hovered close enough to Marianne's torso to graze her skin when she rocked her pelvis, and she could feel Marianne's ragged breath blow across her cheeks. Emily couldn't be closer to her, yet that was what she craved.

She wanted to show Marianne that this was who she really was, the natural progression of the person she'd discovered inside herself in Samui. She wanted to let her know how much she cared about her, how much she owed her—and loved her. How it could be between them if she stayed.

Emily shook that last thought off her, realising it was unfair. She had time to manage her expectations later. Because the way Marianne looked at her, her eyes all but glazing over, tears running from them in steady streams, there was no way she didn't know.

And when she let go, when Marianne's body shivered beneath her, one muscle spasm quickly following the next, it shook Emily to her core. It touched her soul. She took the trip with Marianne, that warm, moist, tingling voyage through flesh and bone that, at the same time, had such an effect on her mind. It was the single most powerful experience of Emily's life.

She let Marianne call the shots, let her gaze up at her with moist eyes and sagging lips before pulling her close, their bodies covered in a layer of sweat.

"You've changed me," Marianne said into Emily's ear. "I want to live again."

Emily pressed her lips into Marianne's tousled hair before pulling out gently. It was an odd sensation, having just fucked another woman like that—the closeness and togetherness it had brought about. As transformative as it had been a few seconds ago, Emily couldn't get the contraption off her quick enough now so she could press her own body against Marianne. She rapidly loosened the straps, slipped out of the harness and tossed it aside.

"I want to live *with you*," she said, after she'd freed herself and rubbed her entire body against Marianne's side. And perhaps it was too soon, maybe even ludicrous, but in that moment, it couldn't have felt more right.

When Marianne didn't instantly reply, Emily pushed herself up on her elbows and scanned Marianne's face. Her eyes were closed, her features relaxed, her limbs sunk into the duvet. It was as at peace as Emily had seen her. She still couldn't believe Marianne was here, in her bed—she almost wanted to reach for the toy again, as if needing to examine evidence.

She planted a soft kiss on Marianne's cheekbone. Marianne opened her eyes in response. A single tear slid along her temple, down onto the pillow.

"Come here," she said, and cradled her arm around Emily's neck, pulling her close.

Emily rested her head on Marianne's chest, just above the swell of her breast. She felt more like home than ever in her flat.

"I guess I'd better start by informing my family of my new lifestyle though," Emily backtracked a little because she fully realised that, just because the moment felt right for her, it wouldn't necessarily be the same for Marianne. "Now that you're here, I feel as if I can really do that, whereas before it was more of an abstract notion."

"Do it when you're ready. You can't force these things." Marianne pulled her close, her fingers travelling across Emily's back. "And even posh Holland Park families have feelings. I've been there, so I know."

"How did your parents react?" *All the questions we have yet to ask each other.*

"Well," Marianne chuckled. "Considering the fact that I always categorically refused to wear a dress or a skirt whenever I was home from school—gosh, these ghastly uniforms they made us wear—and, as a teenager, my room was decorated with pictures of old female movie stars like Ingrid Bergman and Lauren Bacall, it didn't come as that much of a surprise, I suppose." She sighed, her chest heaving up and down. "There were the usual questions. Are you sure? Have you given boys a fair chance? And concerns, of course. Will she ever be happy? How will the world treat her? Because, in the end, no matter where you're from, most parents just want their children to be happy. And once they get past the fact that their child's happiness will not exactly align with their expectations, they find a way to accept it." Marianne's hand had trailed all the way back up to Emily's hair, twirling strands of it around her fingers. "And I was happy. For a long time, I was so happy. Ingrid didn't come from the same background as me, but as soon as my father set eyes on her, he saw what I saw." Marianne's voice broke a little, but she recovered. "If your family is half decent, and I assume they are, having brought up someone as loving and kind as yourself, they'll come round."

"Loving and kind, huh?" Emily's lips found the delicate spot beneath Marianne's ear. "How about irresistibly sexy and naturally adept at wielding a strap-on?"

Marianne giggled and turned on her side, facing Emily. "There's that, but I wouldn't stress these particular details when coming out."

"Will you come with me?" Emily's heart pounded in her chest. "When I tell them."

Marianne shook her head. "I can't do that, baby." Emily's stomach tightened. "Put yourself in their shoes for a second. You break off your engagement, escape to Thailand and come back with a woman more than fifteen years your senior. Sometimes, it's better to minimise the shock."

"It just... I don't know. Somehow, I suspect they'll have an easier time accepting it if you're there. If they can see for themselves that lesbians are not social outcasts and—"

"Ahum," Marianne interrupted her.

"You know what I mean."

"This is something you'll have to do on your own, babe."

MARIANNE

Marianne rang the bell to her parents' house. She hadn't called beforehand and they didn't know she was in town. She'd come to London for Emily and no one else, but she could hardly ignore them after advising Emily on how to handle her own family: with respect, no matter what. Something Marianne had failed to do miserably over the past five years.

As the door slowly creaked open, Marianne wondered how many more times on this trip she'd have to say, "Surprise."

Nearing seventy, her dad still stood regal. His hair had all but gone snow white and it curled to the side of his scalp in long, unkempt wisps, making him look every bit the distracted professor he was.

"Darling, is that you?" He blinked his eyelids open and shut a few times. "Well, do come in." Never one to indulge in very tactile relationships with his children, he curled an arm around Marianne's shoulder and gave her a firm squeeze. The gesture moved her much more than she had anticipated.

"Your mother is out, playing bridge at Ginny's like every Wednesday afternoon, but I'll put the kettle on." He looked a bit out of sorts. No wonder.

"I'll do it, dad. You sit down." Marianne nodded at her father and headed towards the kitchen. No matter how long she went away, some things never changed. The cupboards had been redone and the fixtures refitted, but it was still the kitchen of her childhood, with the same layout and the same gold-plated frames on the wall.

Waiting for the water to boil gave Marianne a few minutes to adjust to her surroundings. She had so many memories in this house, good ones and bad ones. The first time she'd brought Ingrid over for supper. The way she had to drag Ingrid away from never-ending discussions with her father about some sociological phenomenon that, quite frankly, Marianne couldn't even feign interest in. The day she had to tell them what had happened. The time she'd left, soon after, rushing in and quickly out again, for good—she believed.

"How are you, dad?" Marianne handed him a steaming mug of tea.

"Still trying to wrap my head around the fact that you're standing in front of me." A smile tugged at his lips. "Your mother will be in a right state when—"

"I'm coming back, dad." Marianne quickly swallowed away the tears bunching in her throat. "I'm ready."

"You are?" He hid his face behind the mug, but Marianne spotted the tiny drop of moisture forming in the corner of his right eye.

"I'm selling the house in Samui and I…" Marianne hesitated. "I'm coming home."

London had ceased to feel like home the day Ingrid had died. It had instantly turned into a cold, grey, unforgiving place, no matter how many friends and relatives remained, worried and cared about her.

"That's truly wonderful news, darling." Her father could regale an auditorium full of students for an hour on end without failing to grasp their unflinching attention, but when it came to matters closer to the heart, he never had found a way of expressing how he felt with words.

"I met someone and I—I think she needs me here." Marianne had never actively looked for a reason to return, had avoided that altogether really, but now, after seeing the dazzling glint in Emily's eyes when they stood face to face again, it seemed like the most logical course of action ever.

"Your mother will be thrilled. You—you must invite her to supper soon. We'd love to meet... her." Marianne couldn't remember ever having witnessed her father's cheeks redden with pure emotion.

"I will, dad, soon."

"Your mother's bringing back a roast chicken from Sainsbury's. You will stay for dinner, won't you?"

Marianne looked at the man in front of her, kindness flooding her veins. She watched how he battled with bottled-up emotions and she knew she hadn't inherited that particular trait from a stranger. She knew her father understood. "Of course."

She'd made a deal with Emily earlier that day. They'd both go home and share some important news. Emily believed that Marianne's news was simply that she'd come to town unexpectedly. She had no idea that Marianne had made a decision that would change both of their lives.

EMILY

"You're a... a lesbian?" Emily's mother sat with her hands covering her mouth, exactly the way Emily had imagined it. "But... you were with Jasper for five years. I don't understand. How can that be possible?"

Her father put a hand on his wife's knee. They sat in front of her in the sofa. Emily had wisely waited to impart the news until after dinner, lest they choke on their food. She also needed the wine that came with it to loosen her tongue and fortify her courage.

"I mean, how do you know? Did you cheat on him with... with a woman?" Emily's mother blurted out the words. How Emily longed for Marianne's presence. Her mother would never ramble like that in front of a stranger.

"That's enough, Penny." Her father patted her mother's leg again, a bit more forcefully this time as to not miss his point. "Let her talk." He rested his eyes on Emily's, an unexpected understanding brimming in the light blue of them.

"I've always known on some level, I guess. I just never... had the chance to explore. I met someone... a woman, in Thailand. And—"

"Oh, dear god..." A gasp escaped her mother's mouth.

Emily continued undeterred, spurred on by her father's firm glance of reassurance. "Meeting her confirmed what I've known deep down all along. I'm sor—" Emily stopped before apologising. It was simply not something for which she felt she needed to say sorry—a very much overused word in her family.

"This woman lives in Thailand?" her father inquired with his soft baritone that helped him command a court room.

"Yes, but she's here now. She's visiting, I mean, she's from here but she left..." It was Emily's turn to ramble now. "It's a long story."

"Did she... did this woman make you gay?" Her mother was about to reach the suppressed sobbing stage. Emily could tell. She wouldn't actually shed a tear, but every other inflection would be there.

"No, mum. No, of course not. I was—"

"I simply don't understand. You and Jasper were so happy, so gorgeous together. Then you decide to leave him, for reasons no one understood. You go on some journey of self-discovery in Asia and return a lesbian? Something must have happened."

"Look, I understand that you will need some time to let this sink in and that this comes from left field a bit. But nothing happened to me or was done to me. I was always like this, I just didn't realise."

"Robert, do you understand this?" Her mother turned to her father as if he held all the answers instead of Emily.

"I can hardly say I was expecting it." At least, her father addressed her directly. "You have been different since you've come back. More self-assured and goal-oriented. I just figured that trip had done you the world of good."

"Oh, it certainly has." Emily's mind drifted to the day they'd celebrated Marianne's birthday on the beach. It was very difficult to hide the wide grin that wanted to burst all over her face. It was even harder to think back to those days of joy—those days of blissful affirmation of what she already knew—while sitting in front of her parents now, her mother on the brink of tears and her father trying to rationalise it so he could understand. It would be so much easier if they could only see that it was simply a matter of love. Then again, that never mattered a great deal in the Kane family.

Her father cleared his throat. "We respect your choices, Emily. We always will."

Her mother blew her nose discreetly.

"But we need some time to absorb this… news."

Emily took a deep breath. Her father was usually more eloquent, but she understood that this was a shock to their system. She'd come to dinner only to dash their well-practiced, long-rehearsed dreams and expectations. It was only fair to give them some time to adjust. She could hardly expect her non-suspecting parents to invite her lesbian lover to a meal so quickly. Emily was sure though, that if they were only to meet Marianne, it would make things so much easier for them.

"I get it." She looked them both over. Her mother was doing a fairly good job of hiding the perplexed look on her face with her hand, while her father sported his well-worn nothing-can-stop-me lawyer mask. "I just wanted you to be the first to know."

112

"We appreciate that, darling." Her father gave her mother's knee another squeeze, as if wanting to yank her out of her cocoon of sudden misery. "Don't we, Penny?"

Emily witnessed her mother pull herself together. She straightened her back, tucked the handkerchief away in the sleeve of her checkered blazer, inhaled sharply, and rose to her feet.

Emily's stomach knotted at the expectation—the only possible one—that her mother was about to storm out of the room.

"Come here," she said, instead, and opened her arms wide. "Come," she insisted.

Emily pushed herself out of the settee and took a step in the direction of her mother, whose outstretched arms left her nonplussed.

Emily's mother bridged the remaining gap between them and slung her arms around Emily's shoulder. "You're my only daughter. I love you and, frankly, I just want you to be happy."

Tears stung behind Emily's eyes.

"After Jasper, I feared for your happiness so much, sweetheart." She hugged Emily closer. "If this is how it is, then this is how it is."

Emily did something she hadn't done since she was ten years old. She broke out in sobs on her mother's shoulder.

MARIANNE

"She hugged you?" Marianne was confused.

"She hugged me for minutes on end."

"That's a good thing, right?" Marianne had found Emily in quite a state when she'd arrived at her flat.

"Rather disconcerting, if you ask me." Emily stared at her from under her lashes, a small grin playing on her face. "She didn't hug me after I broke up with Jasper. She didn't hug me when I went to say goodbye before my trip."

"She was waiting for the right moment, perhaps." Marianne scooted a little closer. "Saving it for when it mattered most."

"I couldn't have told them if I hadn't known I'd be seeing you tonight, you know."

"That's what you keep telling yourself."

"It's true." Emily scrambled for Marianne's hand. "You give me a strength I don't have when you're not around."

Marianne brought both their hands to her mouth and pressed a kiss on Emily's palm. "I believe it's called sexual satisfaction, babe."

Emily shook her head. "No. It's much more than that."

Marianne adored how Emily could be so intuitively adamant about certain things. She flipped her hand around and found a knuckle with her lips, then another.

"How did it go with your folks?"

Marianne peered at Emily and let a smile take over her face. "Oh, they were very happy with my news."

"What news? That you're in town for another week? Or that you didn't go to see them for days after your arrival because you were hiding out with a girl in her early twenties?"

"Touché." Marianne arched up her eyebrows. "But no, I was referring to another spot of news."

"What?" Emily's fingers squeezed around hers.

She knew it was evil to play with Emily's patience after the night she'd had. "I told them I am moving back to London."

"You... What?"

Marianne's heart leapt in her chest as she scanned Emily's face while her words registered. She sat stock still for an instant, her lips forming a big O.

"I can't, in good faith, leave you here to prance around by yourself now, can I?" Marianne cupped Emily's cheeks with her palms. "Your mother would end up hugging you every day. You'd come out to the world. Chicks would be falling for you in droves."

"Chicks? Come out? What on earth..." Emily stammered. A tear ran down her cheek and Marianne caught it with her thumb. "You're coming back?"

Marianne nodded, overcome with emotion as well. "For you. Yes."

"I—I don't know what to say." Emily placed her hands over Marianne's.

"You don't have to say anything." Marianne stared into Emily's eyes for a moment longer before pulling her in for a soft kiss. "By the way," she said, after locking her gaze on Emily's again, "my parents want to meet you."

"I can't believe this." Tears streaked Emily's cheeks. "You were the one who said I was having unrealistic expectations and that—"

"I know what I said, babe." Marianne sucked her lips into her mouth briefly before continuing. "But coming back to London to see you, instead of revisiting my past, has changed everything. You made it possible for me to experience happiness again here. You made me see the possibility of leading a full life again, with my family, my friends and... you."

"Wait until you meet my family." Emily grinned briefly before her face slipped back into a serious expression. "I love you."

"I love you too."

"Holiday romance, huh?"

"Sometimes, they can be life-changing." Marianne pecked Emily on the lips. "And I guess you were just the right girl at the right time in my life."

"Oh, so it was more destiny instead of me that swayed you?" Emily started pushing Marianne against the back of the sofa.

"No baby, it was definitely you. With these cute dimples in your cheeks and those big blue eyes. And your toys, of course. Let's not forget about those."

"Are you saying it wasn't my sparkling personality that revived you?" Emily straddled Marianne.

"It was everything about you." Marianne's core turned to liquid at the sight of the lust pooling in Emily's eyes.

Emily let her upper body crash against Marianne's chest, her nipples already stiffened to hard pebbles.

"God, you're such a top."

"A what?" Emily asked, her lips already nuzzling Marianne's neck.

"Never mind." Marianne let her hands ride up along Emily's back. "I'll explain later."

Emily's lips reached her ear. "I'm going to make you come so hard you'll want to stay forever."

Marianne believed every word of it.

Emily kissed her way to Marianne's lips. Their tongues met and Marianne held her close, but, as she had learned, it was impossible to hold Emily too long when she was on a mission. And she appeared to be on one now.

Emily freed herself from Marianne's embrace and undid the buttons of her blouse. She wore a deep-red bra underneath and when Marianne's hands rose up to grab at it, Emily swatted them away and pinned them to the sofa for an instant. With her lips drawn into a crooked smile, she brought her hands to her back and unclasped her bra.

Marianne started salivating at the sight of Emily's pert breasts but Emily was in charge—again, case in point—and she knew better than to lean forward and take Emily's hard, rosy nipples in her mouth.

Emily reached for the button of Marianne's jeans next, quickly zipping her out of it as if they'd suddenly landed in the middle of an emergency. She pulled

Marianne's trousers down—knickers and everything—until she sat before her naked from the waist down.

Emily kneeled between her thighs, took each leg and draped it over her shoulders. The last Marianne saw of her face was a wicked grin and a lusty glint in her eyes.

EMILY

Emily was so overwhelmed with emotion, she needed to hide her face somewhere—between Marianne's thighs seemed like the best option.

She inhaled her, by now, familiar sweet-tangy scent while trailing her tongue along the inside of Marianne's upper thigh, first the right one, followed by the left one. So much had happened today, so much had changed, and this was, by far, the only way Emily wanted to celebrate.

She had always believed that the happiness that had surged through her when Jasper had proposed could only be topped by the moment they'd say "I do" to each other, but she couldn't have been more wrong. This was far better. This was who she was, her head buried between another woman's legs, hoarse moans floating in the air around her, nothing else on her mind but giving Marianne an earth-shattering orgasm.

Her tongue darted along the edge of Marianne's trimmed pubic hair, only stopping to allow Emily to blow softly on her engorged pussy lips. Her own clit swelled at the sight, already throbbing violently behind soaked panties.

Marianne's hands had made their way from the spot where Emily had pinned them on the sofa to her hair, tugging at loose strands.

Emily didn't make her wait much longer. She would have if she could, but she ran on emotion and elation and pure lust, and making Marianne beg for it was not on the agenda tonight. She flicked her tongue softly along the length of Marianne's lips.

"Oh baby," the immediate response came from above Emily's head. "Lick me, please."

And Emily did. She let her tongue loose on Marianne's folds, pushing it in as deep as she could, before her lips sucked Marianne's pulsing clit into her mouth.

Emily felt her own pussy release a stream of liquid heat, and she couldn't help herself. She had her hands free, anyway. Frantically, she unbuttoned her pants and let a hand slip into her panties, while the other one held onto Marianne's thigh for support.

While she twirled her tongue around Marianne's clit, her index finger found her own aching bud and she repeated the motion of her tongue with her finger.

To bestow pleasure on Marianne, to have her head buried between Marianne's spread-out legs, was such a turn-on, Emily's hand was quickly flooded with her own juices, her clit as slick and wet as what lay before her.

"Oh god," Marianne groaned, and her pleasure only intensified Emily's. They were held together by one motion. *Flick, circle, flick, circle.* By two body parts of the same person. They were in this together and it was all Emily had ever wanted.

Marianne's legs clasped against Emily's ears, giving her the impression she was in a cocoon of love and lust and burgeoning climaxes.

Emily's orgasm started to build. Her mouth latched on to Marianne's slippery lips as it crossed through her, spurred on by the convulsing movements of Marianne's body, so utterly connected to hers.

"Oh," Marianne moaned, and it was the final straw. Emily came against her own finger, her body sagging against the sofa.

Marianne didn't give her much time to recover. She lifted her legs off Emily's shoulders and pulled at her arms, dragging her back onto the sofa.

Emily luxuriated in Marianne's post-orgasmic embrace, still a little overwhelmed by how extremely right and natural it felt to go down on another woman. How much she wanted it and how much it turned her on.

She lay panting in Marianne's arms, happiness warming her skin.

Archie crawled onto the sofa and joined them. Just like Emily, he'd taken an immediate shine to Marianne.

"What will you do when you come back?" She asked while scratching Archie behind the ear.

"Compete with this pussy for your attention." Their fingers met while stroking Archie's fur.

Emily chuckled, until curiosity got the better of her. "Will you go back into banking?"

Marianne shook her head. "Never." While her one hand remained on Archie, her other found its way to Emily's hair. "I honestly don't know yet."

"I know the perfect place for you to figure it out."

"Oh yeah?" Marianne's fingers had reached the skin of her shoulders, her fingernails hovering over her flesh, leaving goosebumps. "Let me guess." Marianne pushed herself up a bit to plant a kiss on Emily's forehead. "Your Laura Ashley bed?"

"Am I that transparent?" Emily drew her lips into a pout.

"You are to me." Marianne traced a finger from Emily's neck to her chin. "And we haven't even started dating yet."

"I'm Generation Y, infamous for wanting everything here and now. We tend to bypass protocol when we meet a hot woman."

"You can say that again." Marianne tilted Emily's chin towards her. "You'd barely come out of the closet and you were already trying to get into my pants."

"Pants topped by faded black t-shirts sporting eighties icons, to be more specific." Emily leaned in for a kiss. She had expected to find some sort of relief in Asia, or at least, for a little while, an easy way out, but she had never expected to meet her soul mate on a Thai island.

MARIANNE

Marianne's flight from Bangkok to Heathrow had been uneventful fellow passenger and weather wise, but a turbulence had been steadily building in her gut from the minute they had departed. She'd sold the Lodge to Sam who had assured her it would not be bulldozed by land developers. She'd packed up her few belongings, filled a few boxes with the books from her library and shipped them to her parents' house for safekeeping until she found her own place.

Her father, who, despite being retired, still taught heavily attended guest lectures at his university, had promised to enquire about an assistant teaching position in the Economics department. Her mother had insisted that Marianne stay with them when she arrived until she got on her feet but, as expected, Emily would have none of that.

These were all practicalities. Issues that had a tendency to work themselves out. She had made enough money from the sale of the Lodge to live on for a while. And she'd surely be spending her nights in Emily's bed. But, had she, after all was said and done, made the right decision?

Would leaving her cocoon be worth it? Going to London with a return ticket in her pocket was an entirely different experience than arriving with no definite plans for the future. She'd had to shed her armour before boarding the plane. She had to leave it behind, because there was no more room for the old her in London.

A million questions had kept her awake on the flight, despite the bottle of red wine she'd polished off—something that usually did the trick. The holidays were fast approaching—a time of year she always expertly ignored at the Lodge—and for the first time in years she'd have family commitments. Perhaps even a tree. For the first time in years she'd have to give the memories a place. She'd have to catalogue them as the past while looking at the future, at Emily.

It was all easy enough to theorise about, to dream of out loud over Skype, but what would it actually feel like to step into the arrival's lounge and start another new life. Marianne was about to find out.

She collected her luggage and was again baffled by the fact that all the belongings she'd wanted to take fit into two suitcases. She took a deep breath before pushing the trolley through the glass gate.

Spotting Emily instantly in the thick crowd, an unfamiliar warmth engulfed her. Any doubt that had formed on the way over, dissipated at the sight of the blonde curls peeking from under Emily's pink woolen hat.

Don't cry, please, don't cry. But the tears were already rolling down Marianne's cheeks.

They stood facing each other for a few seconds, as if needing to let the moment and all its consequences sink in, before opening their arms and falling into a hug.

"Welcome to your new life," Emily whispered, between sobs, into her ear.

Marianne held her close for long minutes and everything fell away. The people around them. The reasons for doubting her decision. All the things that didn't matter. It was her and Emily now.

Marianne looked down at the grey marble headstone. "I'm back," she whispered. "I've met someone who taught me how to live again." She inhaled the crisp mid-

November air. "I think you'd like her." She reached for the gloved hand dangling next to hers and squeezed it.

"Thank you for bringing me here," Emily said in a soft voice. "It means a lot."

"I'm ready, babe." Marianne faced away from the headstone and looked into Emily's blue eyes. "I'm ready to start living again."

Emily's lips curved into a smile, her cheeks dimpling and her eyes saying all that needed to be said. "You do realise that now you're 'temporarily' staying with me, you'll never be able to move out, right?"

Marianne giggled, but her giggle soon turned into a deep belly laugh. "And you really don't know any of the lesbian jokes, do you?"

The look of vexed indignation on Emily's face was priceless. Marianne pulled her close and kissed her before turning to Ingrid's headstone once more.

She grabbed Emily by the hand and, fingers intertwined, they walked away.

"I did my research on toaster ovens and U-Hauls, you know," Emily said once they'd exited the cemetery.

Marianne chuckled. "I love you," she said, as she drew Emily near and kissed her again. "Maybe we should get another kitten."

ABOUT THE AUTHOR

Harper Bliss has travelled the world in search of sexual satisfaction. She now resides in a hot Asian country and dedicates her time to writing down the stories that have inspired and aroused her.

Harper has had short stories published in anthologies by Xcite Books, House of Erotica and Storm Moon Press. She is the author of the High Rise series and several other novelettes and novellas for Ladylit.

You can connect with Harper via harperbliss.com.

78879345R00078

Made in the USA
Lexington, KY
15 January 2018